MONKEY BUSINESS

books by
leslie margolis

THE ANNABELLE UNLEASHED SERIES
Boys Are Dogs
Girls Acting Catty
Everybody Bugs Out
One Tough Chick
Monkey Business

*

THE MAGGIE BROOKLYN MYSTERIES
Girl's Best Friend
Vanishing Acts
Secrets at the Chocolate Mansion

MONKEY BUSINESS

Leslie Margolis

BLOOMSBURY
NEW YORK   LONDON   NEW DELHI   SYDNEY

First published in the United States of America in September 2014
by Bloomsbury Children's Books
www.bloomsbury.com

Bloomsbury is a registered trademark of Bloomsbury Publishing Plc

For information about permission to reproduce selections from this book, write to
Permissions, Bloomsbury Children's Books, 1385 Broadway, New York, New York 10018
Bloomsbury books may be purchased for business or promotional use. For information on bulk
purchases please contact Macmillan Corporate and Premium Sales Department at
specialmarkets@macmillan.com

Library of Congress Cataloging-in-Publication Data
Margolis, Leslie.
Monkey business / by Leslie Margolis.
pages   cm
Summary: A huge music festival is coming to town, and sixth grader Annabelle and her friends
can't wait to rock out . . . that is if they can come up with enough cash to buy the expensive
tickets.
ISBN 978-1-61963-393-3 (hardcover) • ISBN 978-1-61963-394-0 (e-book)
[1. Friendship—Fiction. 2. Moneymaking projects—Fiction.] I. Title.
PZ7.M33568Mo 2014   [Fic]—dc23   2014005048

Book design by Nicole Gastonguay
Typeset by Westchester Book Composition
Printed and bound in the U.S.A. by Thomson-Shore Inc., Dexter, Michigan
2   4   6   8   10   9   7   5   3   1

All papers used by Bloomsbury Publishing, Inc., are natural, recyclable products
made from wood grown in well-managed forests. The manufacturing processes
conform to the environmental regulations of the country of origin.

For Lucy and Leo,
my favorite monkeys

MONKEY BUSINESS

chapter one
the big move

I woke up early on Saturday morning and panicked—big time!

The problem? I had no idea where I was. Sunlight streamed in through large, pretty but unfamiliar-looking picture windows. It made bright rectangles on the plush peach carpet below.

Peach carpet, I thought. My room doesn't have peach carpet. And it's not this big. Where am I and what am I doing in this place? Was I kidnapped by aliens in my sleep? Am I on a spaceship hurtling toward Mars? And if so, who knew spaceship bedrooms looked so much like human ones? And how come I don't feel as if I'm racing through the stratosphere? Have those aliens already messed with my brain? With their special alien brain scrambler?

I took a deep breath and tried not to panic.

Then I tried to figure out what a special alien brain scrambler would look like.

It would have a lot of wires and blinking lights, I decided as I rubbed my eyes. That's when I realized

I was under my favorite blanket. It's fuzzy, blue, and flannel with pink polka dots. My blanket happened to be on my trusty old bed, which is twin-size with a wooden headboard. The rest of my bedroom furniture was in this strange new place too: desk, bookshelf, and dresser all in a row on the opposite wall. Hmm. All my familiar stuff was there, except my bedroom wasn't what I was used to.

I was seriously confused. I mean, what was going on? This whole morning made no sense. Or, I should say, the whole kidnapped-by-aliens thing was the only explanation. Like, maybe they brought along all my furniture so I wouldn't realize right away that I'd been captured. And if so, the plan kind of worked. I'm probably halfway to Mars by now.

Except for the fact that aliens don't exist. And if they did, what would they want with me, Annabelle Stevens, a short and spunky sixth grader?

I gasped when the following thought occurred to me: maybe Mars needs a whole slew of short and spunky sixth graders. Maybe they wanted to clone me into an all-girl army to fight for peace and justice. Actually, that would be pretty cool. Except, what if they plan to use my clone army for evil purposes, like to conquer Earth? I'd become the face of evil for all humankind. That would be the worst!

It's a good thing human-cloning technology doesn't exist, as far as I know, and like I said before— neither do aliens. So what *was* going on? As the sleep fog from my brain cleared, I remembered what yes-terday was: moving day!

Aha! Now wide awake, I sat up straight. Excitement gurgled in my belly because today was no ordinary day. Big things were happening, and none of them had anything to do with aliens.

Here's the thing: I'm living in a brand-new house and I just woke up in my brand-new bedroom.

Me, my mom, and my stepdad, Ted, plus my scruffy mutt, Pepper, all moved here less than twenty-four hours ago.

Oh, wait. Let me back up a minute and explain a few things. My name is Annabelle Stevens. I'm eleven years old—practically twelve. I am short and skinny with straight blond hair that's long and parted slightly to the left. It's all one length—I don't have bangs. My eyes are brown and my skin is so pale that it burns easily. That's why my mom makes me wear sunscreen every single day. And when we go to the beach, she insists that I wear a hat, even though hats look dorky on me. Plus, they always make my hair even flatter than usual.

I live in Westlake Village, which is outside of Los Angeles, which is in Southern California, which is in the state of California, which is in the United States of America, which is on the continent of North America, which is on the planet Earth, the third planet from the sun.

Our sun, anyway. There could be other solar

systems out there—no one knows for sure. But I guess I've gotten a bit off my subject.

It could be because geography has been on my mind a lot since our big move. Not that the move was so big. That's the funny part. When I left for school yesterday, I lived on Clemson Court. And when I came home from school, I lived on Oakdell Lane.

Today is Saturday and here I am: in a new house, on a new block, in a new neighborhood. We still live in the same town—Westlake. Also, my new house is merely one mile away from my old house. But it feels as if it's a whole world away because we live in an entirely different housing development. Our old neighborhood is called Morrison Woods. Our new neighborhood is called Canyon Ranch.

Another crazy thing about this new house is that my room is literally twice the size of my old room. That's why it felt so weird waking up there this morning. I'm not used to having so much space. Not that I'm complaining. Having a big room is great and the best part is that it's large enough for Rachel, Claire, Yumi, and Emma, my four best friends in the entire universe, to sleep over. And that's exactly what they're going to do tonight!

"Oh, good. You're up," said my mom, poking her head into my room. Her blond curls were piled up in a high ponytail and she was rubbing her belly. She's been doing that a lot lately, because she's pregnant.

Yeah—that's right. That's the other big news in my life. The main reason my family moved to this big new house is that my mom and Ted are going to have a new baby. More important, it means that in a few months I'm going to have a brother or sister. I am dying to know which, but my mom and Ted are insisting on keeping it a surprise.

I wish they'd change their minds and find out so they can tell me. I've even told them they can have the doctor call me and I'll keep it a secret from everyone, but they were not so into that idea. It's too bad, but regardless of whether they're having a boy or a girl I'm going to be a big sister, which is huge! I've been an only child for most of my life. Then last year my mom and Ted got married. Ted has a son named Jason, but he's super-old—twenty-one—and he's away at college. So even though I'm kind of a little sister now, I still feel pretty much like an only child. So it'll be weird to have a baby around—but hopefully weird in a good way.

In the meantime, my mom's belly is so big and round she looks as if she swallowed a regulation-size soccer ball.

"I would say I'm barely awake," I replied, yawning as I peeled off my covers and climbed out of bed. "When I opened my eyes this morning, I didn't know where I was."

My mom laughed. "That same exact thing

happened to me! I guess it'll take a bit of time to get used to the new place."

"Uh-huh," I said. "Um, what's for breakfast?"

"Breakfast burritos! Ted picked them up this morning after his run. And it's a good thing, too. We haven't had time to do any grocery shopping."

Ted goes running almost every single morning. I don't really get why, but I can't complain when there's delicious food involved.

"Awesome. That sounds perfect," I said.

"Good," my mom replied. "You'll want to eat quickly, though, so you can get started on unpacking. This room has to be all set up before your friends come, and you've got a lot of work to do."

"I know, I know," I said, stretching my arms up high over my head and then letting them flop back down with a thump. "But there are so many boxes! Are you sure you can't help?"

My mom laughed. "You're kidding, right? You're lucky you only have to unpack one room. Ted and I are dealing with the rest of the house. And believe me—that's no easy task."

"Okay, fine," I grumbled. "I suppose you have a point."

After my mom left I headed for the bathroom and splashed some cold water on my face. Then I dug around in the large cardboard box labeled BATHROOM SUPPLIES until I found a towel and my toothbrush and toothpaste. I also unpacked everything else in the box—my soap, washcloths, and towels—while I was there. One box down and ten to go!

Next I ran downstairs. Our new staircase was curved in the shape of a C, unlike our old one that had gone simply straight up and down. *I like the curviness*, I decided as I headed for the kitchen. But there was something else I liked even more and I couldn't help but smile as I gazed out at it: our new swimming pool. I'd never had my own pool before, and this particular pool was awesome. It was a big rectangle—perfect for swimming laps or just lounging around on a raft—and the water seemed extra blue and sparkly. All I wanted to do was cannonball in immediately!

Seems like Pepper was enjoying the pool too. He's a black-and-white mutt with about twelve tons of energy. He's super-lovable and mostly well behaved, but he has been known to rip a doughnut straight out of my hands, and sometimes he can't help but jump on me when I come home from school. And speaking of Pepper misbehaving, at the moment he was outside lapping up water from the pool.

"Is he allowed to do that?" I asked my mom, pointing at Pepper through the sliding glass door that led outside.

My mom looked up from her coffee, gazed outside, and frowned. "Probably not. I think the chlorine is bad for his stomach. And his fur could get caught in the drain, which can't be good for the filtration system."

She stood, opened the door, and called for Pepper.

He came right into the kitchen with his tail wagging, probably because he smelled food.

"Morning, Pepper," I said, giving his neck a good scratch. "How do you like our new digs?"

"Please don't say the word 'dig,'" my mom whispered. "I don't want to give him any ideas."

"What kind of ideas?" I asked.

"Well, the last thing I want is for Pepper to dig up the new garden."

I looked at the green grass outside, still totally confused. "What new garden?"

"The new vegetable garden I'm going to plant as soon as I get the inside of this house settled. You know, after I finish my semester of teaching and make sure everything is set up for the new baby and finish reading Proust like I've been meaning to do for the past ten years."

"Oh," I said. My mom has been talking about reading Proust forever, and I don't even know who she is. I took a bite of my burrito. Some salsa dripped onto my chin, and I grabbed a napkin and wiped it off. "Good luck with that."

Pepper whimpered and placed his head in my lap. His scruffy fur was still damp from the pool, so now my favorite baby blue, super-soft flannel pajamas had a giant wet spot. "Ugh, Pep. You smell like a wet dog!" I said, gently pushing his face away from me.

"That's because he is a wet dog," my mom pointed out.

"Um, yeah. Thanks for stating the obvious," I replied. "The problem is, I smell like a wet dog now too."

I went to take another bite of my burrito, but Pepper seemed to have the same idea.

"No jumping," I said firmly as I held my food up over my head. "Pepper, no."

Even though he backed off, he kept staring at me with his big, brown puppy-dog eyes. It was cute for a second, then sad, and then kind of annoying.

"I don't know what's better," I said. "Having a dog begging for my burrito inside the house, or having him drink chlorinated water on the outside."

"I'll take care of him," said my mom, getting up and grabbing Pepper by the collar. "Let's go back outside, buddy." She led him toward the door and put him in the yard.

Once outside Pepper found a red-tailed squirrel to chase.

"Poor animal probably once had a peaceful existence," I said as Pepper barked up at our gigantic avocado tree. "Then the Weeble-Stevens move to town!"

"Well, at least it'll have to get some exercise now," my mom pointed out as she took a small sip of coffee. "That's one chubby squirrel!"

I chewed the final bite of my burrito, crumpled the

wrapper into a tight ball, and looked around. "Where's the trash can?" I asked.

My mom glanced around too, bewildered. "I suppose we haven't unpacked it yet. Why don't you leave it on the table for now? I'll figure something out."

"Okay," I said with a shrug. "I guess I should get going. I've got a lot of work to do."

I headed back upstairs and actually paused at the top of the steps because I forgot which direction my room was in. When I looked to the right, I saw four doors and when I looked to the left, I saw four doors. In our old house, there was no looking to the left at the top of the steps. All the rooms were to the right. This place was literally twice the size of our old house, and it was going to take some time to get used to.

Once I finally figured out where to go—left and all the way to the end of the hall, I kneeled in front of the first box. It was labeled GIRL'S CLOTHES.

"Yup, I would be the girl in this scenario," I thought as I peeled off the tape and pulled open the flaps on top. The box was stuffed full of winter clothes. And since it was only April—not even summertime—I shoved the box into the corner of my closet.

The next two boxes of "Girl's Clothes" were filled with bathing suits, bras, and underwear. I put all my stuff away in the lowest drawer of my dresser. Then I unpacked all my T-shirts and shorts. Dresses came next—I hung them in the closet once I found the hangers at the bottom of the box. And then I unpacked my jeans and pants and leggings. The box after that was labeled MISC., which is short for miscellaneous, which means stuff that doesn't fall into any real category but is decidedly not junk.

I found a few old notes from my friends, a roll of duct tape with purple and red hearts all over it, my science fair project on bugs and their color preferences, a few birthday cards from last year, an old roll of stamps, and a pair of black glasses with a big plastic nose and mustache attached to it.

"How's it going, Annabelle?" my mom asked, poking her head into my room.

I slipped on the glasses. "Who's there?" I asked. "I can't see a thing!"

"Very cute," she said with a laugh. "But I'm glad to see you're making progress. Why don't you use an empty box for the things you don't need anymore?"

"Okay, good idea," I said as I tossed an old red sweatshirt into the closest empty box.

"I thought that was your favorite!" my mom said.

"It used to be, but it has a gigantic hole in the sleeve."

My mom picked up the sweatshirt and inspected the damage. "Oh, that's just along the seam. I can get that fixed if you want."

"Okay, sounds good," I said. "Thanks."

My mom wished me luck and left, and moments later my phone vibrated with a new text.

It was from Oliver Banks, my boyfriend.

Oh, yeah—that was another exciting development in my life. I had a new boyfriend. And having a boyfriend, in general, was brand-new for me. Oliver was my first and he was super-cute and sweet, too. And guess what else? Now that I'd moved, he lived right down the street—only eight houses away.

How r trix? he wrote.

Great!!! I texted back. Then I frowned down at the screen of my phone, wondering if I'd used too many exclamation marks. Three seemed like an awful lot.

Uh-oh . . .

The more I thought about it, the more uneasy I felt. I didn't want to scare Oliver or appear to be yelling at him or anything.

Yikes. I kind of wished there was a way to take one of the exclamation marks back. Ideally two. Or maybe even one exclamation mark was one too many.

If Oliver mentioned them or acted weird, maybe I could tell him my finger had accidentally pressed the button one too many times. Or two too many times—I wasn't really sure which would be more acceptable.

Or maybe it was okay to be excited because moving was exciting. Right?

Except how excited should I allow myself to be? Too much enthusiasm could be construed as weird and/or not cool. It's not that my life is all about appearing cool—it's so not! But at the same time, I didn't want to act like a big dork, or even a little dork. Any kind of dorkiness is best to be avoided. That's a good motto to live by—especially in middle school.

I stared at my phone. Why wasn't Oliver writing me back?

Why, why, why?

Had I already wrecked things?

Did my boyfriend think I was an overenthusiastic dork? Of course he did. No other explanation made sense.

Gah! I couldn't believe how badly I'd messed up. Oliver and I had been officially together for less than two months. And already it was over.

All because of a text.

And not even a whole text.

This was all about the punctuation.

I flopped down backward on my bed and stared up at the ceiling, wishing I could start the day over.

But no—I'd ruined everything with those three exclamation marks. This was the beginning of the end!

chapter two
the trouble with texting

Sometimes I had a tendency to overreact. And maybe this was one of those times, but in my defense, I'd only had my phone for a few months— and my boyfriend for less time than that. I wasn't always up on the etiquette when it came to both Oliver and my phone.

After another thirty seconds of agony I decided to give Oliver a call so I could explain that my fingers had slipped and I had only meant to use one exclamation mark. Except when I began dialing, Oliver texted me back.

Awesome!!!! With four—count 'em, four—exclamation marks. I breathed a sigh of relief. Obviously, I was in the clear. We were equally enthusiastic. No, actually he was 25 percent more enthusiastic than I was, which meant I was more than in the clear. If anyone examined the evidence, they would know that Oliver was the more enthusiastic one in our relationship. Unless he used all those exclamation marks to make fun of *my* use of exclamation marks . . .

Need help unpacking? he asked next.

I smiled down at my phone in relief. Oliver was being sincere—I was sure of it. As much as I wanted to, I resisted the urge to hug my phone, because that would have been just weird. Still, I felt all gushy toward Oliver and wished I could give him a real hug. Unpacking is dull, dull, dull. That Oliver offered to help merely confirmed the fact that I seriously had the sweetest boyfriend in the world.

I wish—Mom says I can't have anyone over until my room is finished, I texted back.

He replied with a sad face.

Tomorrow! I typed, with one exclamation mark because I was cool like that.

I kept unpacking, now with a huge grin on my face. The next box was labeled PLUSH, and when I tore open the cardboard flaps, a giant stuffed unicorn tumbled out. This made me smile. "Hey, Zilda," I said as I picked her up and stared into her purple-with-sparkles eyes. "I haven't seen you in ages."

Okay, yes, it could be seen as dorky, talking to my stuffed animal, but it was no biggie because I was alone in my room. Also, I hadn't seen Zilda or the rest of my stuffed animals since forever. Yet here they all were! Curious and excited, I dumped the entire box onto my floor.

I stared at every single animal I'd ever owned, with the exception of Snowball, my favorite mouse ever, who I'd insisted on taking to Disneyland when I was six because I wanted her to meet Mickey even though my mom warned me she'd probably get lost. Guess what? My mom was right. Snowball disappeared in Adventureland—an hour before we even spotted Mickey—and I haven't seen her since. It still kind of makes me sad. Back when it happened my mom told me animals that get lost at Disneyland are lucky because they get to stay at "the happiest place on Earth" forever. And I knew she was making it up, even at the time, but I still liked to picture Snowball and Mickey riding Alice's teacups together when the park was closed at night.

Anyway, back to the stuffed animals that didn't get left behind at theme parks . . . When I was younger, I slept with each and every one of them at my side. It was a rule, like, I wouldn't go to bed without them—this despite the fact that every morning when I woke up, half the animals would be on the floor and others would be stuck in the narrow space between the wall and my bed.

It'd been a lot of years since then. And it was fun to reconnect with old friends. I decided to sort them all by type.

Buttons, my favorite beat-up old stuffed hippo, sat at the top of the pile. My grandmother gave her to me when I was born. She's fat and blue with blond braids and sparkly red shoes. Not my gran—she's skinny and white with gray hair. I was talking about Buttons, who used to have actual gray buttons sewn onto her chest, as if her body were a cardigan sweater, but all the buttons fell off. Then a few months ago Pepper mistook her for a chew toy. And the results weren't pretty. Still, Buttons was a keeper. I placed her on the top shelf of my bookcase.

Then I turned to the rest of the animals. I had three more unicorns; two elephants; one giant goldfish; eight dogs; three cats; four rabbits; five monkeys; a hedgehog; one purple, three-eyed Uglydoll; and two turquoise one-eyed Uglydolls—twin Uglies! I forgot about how cute they were. I put all the Uglydolls on my bookshelf and then went back to sorting. Turns out I also had a complete set of Sesame Street puppets: Bert and Ernie, Big Bird, Grover, Mr. Snuffleupagus, Cookie Monster, Elmo, and Animal.

I wasn't sure what to do with them. I didn't want them on my bed—that was for sure. I was going to be twelve in a few weeks. I was way too old to sleep with a gazillion stuffed animals.

But even though I didn't want to sleep with my stuffed animal collection anymore, I couldn't fathom parting with it for good. No, the animals were all way too important to be hawked at some garage sale. So what was I supposed to do?

I packed them up and shoved the box into the hall. I'd talk to my mom about it later. Maybe I could save them for my new brother or sister. Not to keep—just to borrow for a few years. Babies love stuffed animals! And my baby brother or sister would have an instant collection. Lucky kid!

I unpacked three more boxes, feeling like the greatest future big sister in the world. I put all my schoolbooks on my bookshelf and placed my spare printer paper in a stack on one corner of my desk, and my socks in my sock drawer.

Then I took a quick break for lunch and got back to work.

I found a bunch of stuff to give away—some sneakers that were too tight. The flats I wore to my mom and Ted's wedding that were never comfortable in the first place, and a white T-shirt with a mysterious red stain on the middle of it. And when I finally finished dealing with all the boxes, my stomach was growling, so I wandered downstairs. Luckily, my mom was just coming inside with a big takeout bag from Gino's, our favorite Italian restaurant.

"Hungry?" she asked.

"Starving!" I told her.

She laughed. "Good. Me too."

Ted came in behind her carrying two big bags filled with groceries. "Hi, Annabelle. You've been quiet all day," he said. "I kept meaning to check on you to make sure you weren't trapped under an avalanche of boxes."

"It's all good," I said, sitting down at the kitchen table. "And I'm finally finished!"

"Well done. The house is coming together so fast," Ted said as he sat down next to me. "And don't worry,

Annabelle. We'll get your basketball hoop installed by the end of the week. Tomorrow, even, if I can track down the hardware."

"Excellent!" I said. "And what about the trampoline?"

Ted grinned at my mom. "I thought the trampoline was going to be a surprise," he said.

My mom turned bright red. "It was," she said carefully. "Hmm. I wonder who told her."

We all laughed because the answer was obvious. Anyone who knows my mom knows that she's terrible at keeping secrets.

"I was surprised when I found out you were getting me a trampoline," I said as diplomatically as possible. "And I'll be thrilled once it's here. You guys are amazing parents!"

"Spoken like someone who really wants a trampoline," said Ted.

"We'll order it as soon as we unpack the house," my mom promised.

"My room is done," I said. "Remember?"

"I guess that means you can invite your friends over," said my mom.

"Oh, I already texted them twenty minutes ago," I said. "As soon as I started on my last box."

"You are exceedingly efficient," said Ted.

I stood up and looked out at our backyard. "I was hoping the trampoline would be set up already so we could bounce tonight. And I know just the spot for it—at the deep end of the pool. I'll bet I can figure out how to do a reverse flip into the water."

"Um, having you fall off the trampoline and crack your head open is my biggest nightmare," said my mom. "So keep talking like that and the trampoline may never arrive."

"Sorry. Never mind," I said quickly.

The doorbell rang as I was finishing my sandwich. "I'll get it," I said, jumping up and then moving my dishes into the sink.

Pepper beat me to the entryway and barked like crazy. He always went nuts when someone came over—don't ask me why.

I raced toward the door and tried to stop short but ended up skidding in my socks halfway across the entryway. "Yikes, our new floors are slippery," I called to no one in particular.

Through the stained glass window in the middle of our door I spied three figures: a tall blurry person with long red hair who could only be Claire; a short blurry person in a blue Dodgers cap with short black braids sticking out on either side who had to be Yumi; and a medium-size, slightly slouchy person with long brown hair parted in the middle who had to be Emma.

I opened the door with a big grin on my face. "Hey, guys!" I said. "You're right on time. Welcome to my new house!"

"Thanks for having us over!" said Claire, coming in and giving me a big hug. "This is so exciting."

"I'm missing the second half of the Dodgers game for this," said Yumi. "But it's totally worth it."

My friends all dropped their stuff inside and then looked around.

"Your entryway is so fancy," Yumi said, gazing up at the crystal chandelier overhead.

"I'm so happy we live closer now," said Emma, flashing me the screen of her phone, which was on its timer setting. "It took me ninety-five seconds to walk here, and I wasn't even hurrying."

"That's great! Let's go upstairs and I'll show you my room," I said, grabbing one of Claire's suitcases. She'd brought two, which was so Claire. She changed outfits at least three times a day. At the moment she had on a purple-and-blue paisley long-sleeved shirt and cutoff jean shorts with a rainbow peace sign embroidered on both front pockets. Most likely she'd done the embroidery work herself.

"Rachel texted to tell me she'd be late," said Yumi. "She's stuck at her grandparents' house for dinner tonight and she couldn't get out of it."

"No worries," I said, leading them upstairs and into my brand-new bedroom. "I haven't had a chance to put up my posters yet, but here we are. . . ." I spread out my arms.

"Wow, your room is huge," said Claire as she

looked around. "And check out your closet! I dream of having a walk-in closet!"

"You do," said Emma.

"I mean one of my own—and a room that I don't have to share with Olivia."

Claire has an older brother and sister. They're eighth-graders and twins named Olivia and Charlie.

"I like Olivia," I said. "She's cool and super-sweet."

"She is," said Claire. "As far as sisters go, I'm lucky. She never minds when I borrow her clothes and she doesn't hide her diary that well, so I always know what's going on with her."

"You read her diary?" I asked, shocked.

"Shh!" Claire said, raising her finger to her lips. "Let's not publicize that fact."

"You kind of just did," said Emma.

"Right—but I'm trusting that the information won't leave this room," said Claire.

"Got it," I said with a nod. Then I thought about this for a moment. "Do you think my future baby brother or sister is going to read my diary?" I wondered.

"Probably," said Claire, wiggling her eyebrows. "So consider yourself warned."

"That's going to be so annoying!" I cried. Then I thought about it for a minute. "Oh, wait. Except I don't actually have a diary."

Everybody laughed, and Emma said, "Make sure you don't start one now."

Then Claire unzipped her orange duffel bag and pulled out a pair of white Converse sneakers. On each side were hand-painted little black-and-white dogs. They looked sort of like Pepper in miniature.

"Those are so cute!" I said.

"Glad you like them because I made them for you," Claire said.

I gasped. "This day keeps getting better and better and it's not even my birthday!"

"This is your housewarming present," said Claire. "You'll need the new shoes because you'll be walking farther to get to and from school from now on."

"True," I said, giving Claire a quick hug. "Thank you. You're the best."

Then I looked more closely at the sneakers and said, "You did an amazing job!"

"Thanks. It was easy," Claire said proudly as she tucked her hair behind her ears. "Fun, too, since Pepper is the most adorable puppy."

Right when she said his name, Pepper hopped into her lap. Claire giggled and scratched him behind his ears. "Hi, cute guy!"

He licked her face in response.

"Thanks for making me look bad," said Yumi. "I didn't bring a thing!"

"Neither did I—except for my sparkling personality," said Emma as she batted her eyelashes at us.

We all giggled.

"Oh yeah, I have that too," said Yumi.

"That's certainly enough," I assured them as I stepped out of my flip-flops and then sat down to try on the new high-tops.

"They fit perfectly," I said.

"You should probably wear them with socks or you'll get blisters," Emma pointed out.

"I guess so." I crossed my room to my dresser drawer and pulled out a pair of white tube socks with chunky red and blue stripes.

"Those are so retro," said Claire. "Perfect for the Converse."

"I'm glad you approve," I said as I pulled them on. "And thanks again. I'm so excited to have another one-of-a-kind Claire original."

"Can I commission a pair?" asked Yumi. "Maybe blue shoes that say, 'Go Dodgers' on each side?"

"Sure," said Claire. "I'm picturing it now—a little baseball with red stitching and letters all in silver. What size shoes do you wear?"

"Six," said Yumi.

Claire pulled out her phone and plugged in the information.

Then suddenly Pepper shot out of the room and down the steps, barking all the way.

Seconds later the doorbell rang.

"Oh, that must be Rachel!" I said, jumping up and following Pepper to the front door. "I should lock up Pepper."

Rachel is allergic to dogs—they give her hives.

And the only reason she was able to sleep over tonight was because I'd promised we'd keep Pepper out of my room and away from her in general.

I ran to the front door just as Ted opened it. Rachel stood in the doorway with her trusty red backpack slung over one shoulder, and her green sleeping bag tucked under her opposite arm.

"Hold on. Let me put Pepper outside," I said, grabbing him by the collar.

"I'll take him," said my mom. "And hi, Rachel. We'll keep him away. Don't worry."

"Thanks," Rachel said. Her eyes seemed red and puffy already.

"Wow, you really are allergic, huh?" I asked.

"What?" asked Rachel, blinking at me. "Oh. Yeah."

"Hi, Rachel. Now let's see," said Ted, counting on his fingers. "That's one, two, three, four of you. Annabelle's friends have all arrived, which means the five musketeers are together again!"

"I don't even know what that means," I said. "But please don't say it again."

"You've got it, boss," Ted said with a smile and a salute.

I stared at him silently as if to say: "please don't embarrass me." Except obviously it was too late!

"I'll take that as my cue to leave," said Ted as he backed away. "Have fun, girls!"

"Sorry I'm late. I got stuck at dinner with my grandparents," said Rachel as she walked inside and readjusted her rainbow-striped ski cap. It'd been pretty hot out these days, but Rachel doesn't wear her ski cap to stay warm. She wears it to keep her curly brown hair under control because, according to her, it gets too frizzy. Especially in the spring and summer, when the humidity index increases. So yes, when winter ends and most people are putting away their jackets and boots and scarves and things, that's the exact moment when my best buddy Rachel breaks out her ski caps.

"It's okay," I said. "You didn't miss a thing. Everyone just got here."

"Come on upstairs, Rachel," Yumi called from the top of the steps. "You should see Annabelle's new room!"

Rachel followed me up the steps and into my bedroom. She took one look around and exclaimed, "Wow!"

Then she dropped her backpack and sleeping bag to the ground and narrowed her eyes at me. "This whole house is ridiculous, Annabelle. Please don't tell me you're going to turn into a Canyon Ranch snob now."

Silence fell over the room. My friends and I stared at Rachel, wide-eyed.

A Canyon Ranch snob? What was Rachel even talking about?

chapter three
the panda parade

That silent moment between me and my friends seemed to last for a long, long time. No one seemed sure what to say or do. Moments before, we'd been having the best time. Then Rachel showed up and accused me of being a snob? Not cool! Everyone seemed too shocked to say anything, myself included.

Eventually Claire broke the silence. "Ha-ha. Very funny, Rach," she said.

My other friends giggled too, but it all seemed forced. Like they wanted to believe Rachel was joking but they weren't quite sure.

I wished I could have joined them, but it felt too weird. Almost like I'd be laughing at myself. Because what Rachel said? Maybe she'd been *trying* to make a joke. But it wasn't funny. Not the least bit. Still, I felt like I had to say something. Plus, Rachel was staring at me, and her big brown eyes seemed colder than usual. She looked as if she wanted to pick a fight. Or was at least putting the bait out there with her comment and waiting to see if I'd take it.

Was I going to take it?

"That's a good one," I said. Except my voice sounded harsh too. I couldn't hide my anger and I didn't want to. I was mad at Rachel for ruining my good mood and for putting me in this awkward position. It was as if we were suddenly in a showdown, but what were we fighting over, exactly?

Rachel didn't respond or even look at me, and everyone seemed to feel the tension in the room.

"Let's talk about something else," Emma said gently. She turned to Yumi. "What's the latest with Nathan?"

"We're back together," said Yumi.

"That's great!" said Claire, clapping her hands. She was probably happy for Yumi *and* relieved that we'd changed the subject. I know I was!

"It's great if it's what you want," said Rachel. "Last time you guys broke up you said that was it."

"I know," said Yumi, sighing in a dreamy way as she stared off into the distance, probably imagining her and Nathan walking on a beach at sunset. "But he's the perfect guy. Or at least he would be if only we lived in the same time zone."

Nathan is Yumi's on-again-off-again long-distance boyfriend. He lives in Michigan. They met in Hawaii over Christmas vacation when they were both visiting their grandmothers, who live in the same condo complex.

"And if you'd seen him in person more than once in your whole entire life," Rachel said.

This was true, but the way Rachel said it seemed kind of harsh and overly critical. Maybe she was in that kind of mood. I watched Yumi's reaction and waited for her to say something, but she didn't even blink.

"It seems ridiculous sometimes," said Yumi, all light and sincere. "But the thing is—we are so perfect together! We have the best Skype dates and he texts me almost every single day. Plus, we convinced our parents to take us to Hawaii at the same time this summer, so at least I'll get to see him again."

"Wow!" I said. "That's really great news!"

"It's all so romantic," Claire said with a sigh. "I wish I had a boyfriend."

None of us said anything. Even though I looked down at my feet, I could tell everyone was stealing glances at me. Claire used to like Oliver. Things got kind of complicated for a while, but it all worked out. At least for me—I got Oliver, and Claire is still one of my best friends.

Yumi sat down on my window seat and looked out the window. "You have a great view of the swimming pool."

"I know," I said. "Do you guys want to go in?"

"I don't have my bathing suit," said Yumi.

"You can borrow one," I said.

"I don't have mine, either," said Emma.

"You can borrow one too," I said.

"Do you have a fourth?" asked Claire.

I thought about this for a moment. I'd just unpacked all my bathing suits this morning. I had the navy blue one-piece with white polka dots, the pink-and-green-striped tankini, and a black racing suit with orange-and-yellow flames.

"Sorry, guys. I've only got three suits. I wish I'd have thought of this before—I would've asked you all to bring your own."

"You should have!" said Claire. "It's so warm out tonight and I'd love to swim."

"This is my first swimming pool," I said. "I suppose I don't have the etiquette down."

"You'll learn," said Emma. "Or you'll get more bathing suits."

"Or both," said Yumi with a shrug.

"I already went swimming this morning anyway," Rachel said with a yawn. "Of course, my pool isn't as fancy as yours is."

Claire laughed but no one else did.

Know why? Because what Rachel had said wasn't even funny.

I stared at Rachel, wondering if this was supposed to be another one of her bad jokes. She seemed to be kidding but at the same time, not. But what reason could she have had for being mad at me? I hadn't done anything wrong.

Suddenly someone knocked on the door.

"Who is it?" I called, happy for the interruption.

"Probably your butler," Rachel said.

I opened my mouth to argue with her, but before I had a chance to speak, Ted called, "Annabelle, this is your butler."

As my friends broke out into giggles, I ran to the door and opened it. "Hey, are you eavesdropping?" I asked.

Ted laughed and held up his hands in surrender. "Guilty as charged, but it was an accidental eavesdrop. I promise. I just got to your door."

"Okay," I said. "We'll have to be more careful next time."

"You mean like speak in code?" asked Ted.

I rolled my eyes and tried closing the door on him, but he blocked it with his hand. "Wait! I actually have a reason for being here."

"What is it?" I asked.

"Jean and I were wondering if any of you were in the mood for ice cream sundaes," Ted said.

"Yes!" shouted my friends.

Ted stumbled back, pretending like he was literally bowled over by the force of our enthusiasm. (Told you my stepdad was corny!) "Great. Ice cream is downstairs. Annabelle's mom got way too much so I hope you're all—"

None of us waited around for Ted to finish his

sentence. We'd already pushed past him and sprinted downstairs to the kitchen.

"There is nothing more exciting than a sundae bar!" Claire exclaimed, delighted, once we were gathered in the kitchen in front of the display.

I was excited to see that my mom and Ted had gone all out. There was hot fudge and caramel, slivered almonds and pistachio nuts, M&M's and Reese's Pieces, and even crumbled Kit Kat bars. Also? Three different kinds of ice cream: chocolate, vanilla, and strawberry.

"This is better than what they have at Pinkberry," said Yumi. "Thanks, Jean."

"Well, this is a special occasion," said my mom. "The first time all four of you have spent the night. We want to make sure you come back again. Okay?"

"Oh, we'll be back," said Emma, popping a blue M&M into her mouth. "All you have to do is serve us candy. We're totally predictable that way."

"Yeah, and you may have a hard time getting us to leave now," Claire added.

Making sundaes cheered us all up, and I tried to forget about Rachel's weird comments. Maybe she really was only joking about the whole thing—teasing me about being a snob now. Except Rachel had never teased me before today. She doesn't have that kind of sense of humor. Also? She's the kind of girl who always says what's on her mind. So I wasn't sure exactly what was going on. . . .

"Hey, Jean. Is there any whipped cream?" asked Rachel.

"Of course!" said my mom, opening up the fridge and handing Rachel a tub of freshly whipped cream.

"You don't have the spray kind that comes in a can?" she asked.

"Sorry," said my mom.

"That's okay," said Rachel, frowning at the bucket. "This will do."

"Want a cherry?" asked my mom, offering her the jar and shaking it gently so the bright red cherries floated around in the syrup.

"No, thanks," Rachel said as she spooned the whipped cream onto her ice cream. "I'm on a diet."

We laughed again. And then we all got really quiet as we focused on constructing the perfect sundae.

I started with a scoop of vanilla and used M&M's to make eyes, a nose, and a mouth. Then I piled it all high with whipped cream.

"That's beautiful," said Emma as she licked some chocolate ice cream off her finger. "It's like that old-fashioned hairstyle. The one that Marge Simpson has."

"A bouffant," I said, drizzling caramel sauce on top of my sundae's head. "Thanks, but it's supposed to be a ten-gallon hat. This sundae's name is Hank."

"Why Hank?" asked Emma.

"Why not?" I shrugged.

Everyone else decided to give their sundaes names and faces too.

"Mine is Nathan," said Yumi. "I'm giving him blue M&M's for eyes, exactly like the real, live Nathan."

"Oh, he's so dreamy!" Claire said in this funny high-pitched voice that made all of us crack up.

"That's kind of weird, eating an ice cream sculpture of your boyfriend," I said. "What if it's actually like a voodoo doll and you're hurting him?"

"You're calling me weird when you're the one who named your ice cream in the first place?" asked Yumi.

"Okay, good point," I had to admit. "Except I made up a name."

"My sundae is named Eleanor, after Eleanor Roosevelt," Emma said, glancing at Rachel. "What are you calling yours?"

She frowned down at her sundae. "I'm leaning toward Gertrude, but hold on a second." She took a large spoonful of sundae and popped it into her mouth. "Mmm. Yeah—she definitely tastes like a Gertrude."

Everybody giggled.

"Hey, you haven't named your sundae yet," I said to Claire, who was silently eating her dessert in the corner.

"I can't," said Claire. "It goes against my basic philosophy of life. I always say I'm a vegetarian because I would never eat anything with a face, so if I give my sundae a face, he or she will become personified and it'll be like cannibalism."

I looked at Claire, trying to figure out if she was serious or not. Sometimes it was hard to tell with her.

But then Emma cracked up and Claire did too, and soon we were all practically collapsing in fits of giggles.

"You girls are hilarious," said my mom. "Ted, do you know where the camera is?"

"Oh no," I said. "No pictures."

I'd just realized I had gotten so busy unpacking I forgot to take a shower today. I wasn't going to admit it out loud, and I definitely didn't want photographic evidence of my mistake.

"Come on," said my mom. "How else are we going to commemorate the new move?"

"By simply moving in and going on with our lives like regular people," I suggested.

"You're going to love these pictures one day," Ted said as he handed my mom their camera. "Plus, don't you want to show your future brother or sister what your life was like before he or she arrived?"

I glanced at Ted, worried. "Are you saying I'm not going to have any sleepovers once the new baby is here?"

"We're not saying that," said my mom, raising the camera. "Smile, everyone. And hold up your sundaes, too. I'd like to document these before they disappear."

"Better hurry," Ted said.

"Wait, Gertrude's eyes fell off," said Rachel, reaching into the pistachio bowl for a new set.

"Okay, now are you all ready?" she asked.

My friends nodded and posed and then finally, after my mom took a bunch of pictures, I told her, "Enough is enough! These are melting and we've gotta eat!"

We sat down again and ate, and by the time we were done with the sundaes and had cleaned up and stacked our dishes in the new dishwasher, the sun was down.

This was good because my mom had this rule that I wasn't allowed to watch TV in daylight, even on special occasions like my birthday or Christmas or when I had a bunch of friends over. She's convinced that as long as the sun is up everyone in the world should be doing something athletic or creative or educational or work-related, rather than sitting around like a lump in front of the TV. (Her words, not mine.)

She didn't care that sometimes I was tired after a long day at school. Sometimes sitting around like a lump was all I had the energy to do.

But we didn't have to have that argument again today because it was already dark outside. The timing was perfect because Claire had brought over one of her favorite DVDs—a movie called *Pitch Perfect*. And the rest of us had never seen it, so we all flopped down on the dark green leather couch in the den.

"Uh-oh," I said, staring at the three remotes that went with the brand-new flat-screen television my mom and Ted had bought for the new house. "I don't know how to use this. Hold on."

I ran into Ted's office, where he was unpacking a bunch of boxes of books.

"I don't know why I moved with a set of encyclopedias when everyone always looks up stuff on the Internet now," said Ted. "I should really give them away. Or maybe recycle them."

"Yeah—I don't think I've ever used one of those in my whole entire life," I said. "Except as a step stool when I needed to get something from the highest shelf and couldn't find our ladder."

"That is telling," said Ted.

"Um, can you help us with the TV?" I asked.

"Sure." Ted stood up, brushed the dust off his hands, and followed me into the living room where my friends waited patiently.

Claire was braiding Emma's hair into one long French braid. Rachel was picking blue nail polish off her thumbnail as Yumi flipped through Ted's copy of *Sports Illustrated*.

"Sorry, girls," he said. "We're experiencing some minor technological difficulties with the new TV and cable system. I should be able to sort it out, though."

He tried to put in the DVD and press play, but nothing happened. After turning the machine off and on again and trying a bunch of buttons, he said,

"Looks like one of these cables is plugged in wrong or maybe the entire outlet is dead. This could take some time, so why don't you girls watch something on regular TV tonight?"

"Okay," I said, glancing down at the remotes again. "And how do I do that?"

Ted grinned and handed me the skinny silver remote. "Just press power and then punch in the channel you want. Our cable is the same so you don't have to learn new numbers."

"Phew!" I grabbed the remote and went straight to Nickelodeon. A *Victorious* rerun was on.

"Oh, I love this one!" I said.

"I've never seen it," Yumi said.

Rachel shushed us, which seemed pretty rude, but no one commented or even looked at her twice.

At the commercial break my favorite song came on. "Ain't Wasting No More Tears for You" by Josie DeBecker. Except it wasn't the whole song or music video. It was a commercial for something called the Panda Parade, which, we soon learned, was an all-weekend-long music festival in Indio, California.

"Hey, where's Indio?" I asked my friends.

"It's near Palm Springs," said Yumi.

"Oh," I said, staring at the TV. "And where's Palm Springs?"

Emma laughed. "It's about two, two and a half hours from here. East. Like in the desert."

"Oh, that's close," I said, turning back to the commercial, intrigued. "Kind of."

"It's not close enough to ride our bikes, but it's close enough that we don't have to take a plane to get there," Rachel said, looking up from her nails. "I know because we went last year for spring break. The drive took forever, especially since Jackson won a bet and we had to listen to his music the whole way, but it was worth it in the end because we rented a condo that had a really great pool and a hot tub. Plus, it was right on a golf course."

"Do you know how to golf?" asked Yumi.

"No," said Rachel. "But I like riding in golf carts, and our condo came with one. Except my dad hid the keys the whole time because he was afraid Jackson would try to go for a joyride."

Jackson is Rachel's older brother. He's in the eighth grade—two years older than we are, yet still not as mature.

"That concert does sound really fun," said Claire. "I can't wait until I'm old enough to go to music festivals."

Suddenly Rachel's eyes got bright. "Maybe we are old enough."

"You think?" asked Claire.

"I've been to concerts before with my parents," said Emma. "Maybe we could all go together if a couple of them agree to chaperone."

"I love that idea!" I said.

Rachel sat up straighter. "Maybe we could rent the same condo and go for the weekend. There's room for all of us—I don't mind doubling up."

"I don't mind sleeping in the bathtub if it means I get to go to the Panda Parade," said Claire. "I've always wanted to see Taylor Swift live."

Emma pulled out her phone and looked up the concert. "You guys—the festival is happening the weekend of July Fourth. And it's a benefit concert for endangered panda bears."

"I was wondering why it was called the Panda Parade," said Yumi.

"Listen to this lineup," said Emma, still reading from her phone. "Josie DeBecker, Taylor Swift, Katy Perry, the Lobster Lips, Lorde—"

With each new name, we squealed.

"I am obsessed with Lorde," said Claire. "She is definitely one of my favorite artists now."

"I know," said Yumi. "I just got her new CD, and I can't stop listening to it."

"Someone told me she's still in high school," said Claire.

"That's crazy. If I were famous, I'd totally drop out of school," said Rachel.

"The Lobster Lips are pretty awesome too," I said. "Jason introduced me to them over Christmas break, and now I listen to them practically every single day. I can't believe there are so many great bands playing all at once."

"'And hundreds more and lots of surprises,'" said Emma, reading the concert description off her phone. "This festival is going to be huge. There are five different stages."

"I don't even know what that means," said Rachel. "But I'm excited!"

"I think it means there are tons of bands playing. Lots of headliners and then ones that we've never heard of," said Claire. "Which is so cutting-edge!"

"Hey, Mom!" I ran into the kitchen to find my mom and Ted eating sundaes of their own. I told them all about the Panda Parade. We don't already have plans for the Fourth, right? So can I go? Please, please, please can I?"

My mom stared at me, a bemused expression on her face.

"Please take this seriously!" I told her. "This is not a laughing matter."

"I'm not laughing," she said.

"Well, you're about to. I can tell."

"Oh, you know me so well, Annabelle. I am simply smiling because you're so worked up over this, which is great. The thing is, though, Indio is far away. Almost three hours from here."

"More like two hours and forty-five minutes," Rachel called from the living room, where my friends were clearly eavesdropping.

"I know it's far," I said. "That's why we want to go for the whole weekend. We'll just rent a condo." I shrugged. It seemed so simple. Okay, I didn't really know if it was easy to rent a condo or not. The only condos I knew of belonged to grandparents. But the way Rachel had said it, well, it seemed like no big deal.

Except as soon as I'd finished my plea, my mom and Ted both cracked up.

"Hey, you promised you wouldn't laugh!" I said. "And how is that funny?"

"I'm sorry, dear," said my mom. "It's the way you casually talk about renting a condo as if you've done it a million times. . . . Tell you what, though. The concert does sound fun and I'm not saying no. Let me speak with your friends' parents about it and see what they have to say. I'm sure we can work something out."

"Yes!" I pumped my fist.

"I didn't say yes," my mom reminded me.

"I know," I said. "But I have a feeling it's all going to work out."

"We'll see," said my mom. But she was smiling and her tone of voice told me everything was going to be great.

Later that night, after two more episodes of *Victorious*, my friends and I headed upstairs to my room and laid out our sleeping bags.

"That sundae was the best," said Claire.

"Mine was amazing too, except I'm so full, I think my stomach is going to burst," said Yumi.

Emma giggled. "That's the sign it was a good meal. Bursting organs."

"Blech!" I said.

"I'd never guess that this is your first group sleepover, Annabelle. You're very good at it," said Yumi.

"Thanks," I said. "It could be beginner's luck, though."

"First big sleepover," said Rachel. "First time living in a mansion . . ."

"This isn't a mansion," I said.

"Sure it is," said Rachel.

I looked around and shrugged. "It's just a big house. Why are you picking on me? Emma lives in this neighborhood too. And her house is the same exact size. Same goes for Oliver and lots of other kids from school."

"I'm not picking on you. I'm simply stating a fact," said Rachel.

"In a not-exactly-nice tone of voice," I said.

"You're too sensitive. This is my normal voice," said Rachel. "You should be used to it by now!"

"It's not just your voice—it's everything you've said tonight. You're acting way harsh."

"You guys, stop fighting," said Yumi.

"Then tell Annabelle to stop bragging about her new house as if it's some huge crazy deal," said Rachel.

"I'm not bragging," I said. "I never even brought up the house—you did. What is going on with you?"

Rachel stared at me and shrugged.

"Seriously, tell me what you're so mad about," I said.

Everyone watched us. If there were an award for creating the most awkward sleepover moment ever, then Rachel and I would be getting a big fat trophy.

The longer she refused to answer me, the more annoyed I grew. And the more silent the room, the more unbearable it all became. Rachel was totally ruining my sleepover and she wouldn't even tell me why.

"Well?" I asked her again. "What's going on?"

"Nothing," she replied coolly as she smoothed out the wrinkles in her green-on-the-outside and orange-on-the-inside sleeping bag. "I'm not mad at all."

Rachel was a lot of things—smart, funny, frizzy-haired, and good at riding a unicycle—but she was a bad liar. Rachel was clearly angry with me. But why, when I hadn't done anything wrong? I hadn't even done anything different except for moving, and that wasn't even my idea.

chapter four
needed: cold hard cash

Everyone told their parents about the concert when they got home from my sleepover Sunday morning. We all figured it would be a no-brainer. The concert was months away. It was happening over the summer, and we were all going to be around. We just needed our parents to buy us tickets and get a couple of people to drive us there. Unless one of Claire's moms was willing to do it—in which case it would be even easier because her family has a minivan.

But no! Something terrible and *way* more annoying happened. All our parents got together on a conference call and came up with their own crazy idea: we could only go to the concert if we paid for the tickets ourselves. Except it was actually more complicated than that.

My mom and Ted broke the news to me on Monday morning.

"We looked into the concert and the tickets cost a hundred dollars each, which is a lot of money," my mom explained over homemade blueberry pancakes, as if a yummy breakfast would make me digest this terrible news more easily. "And we figure you girls should also contribute toward the other expenses."

"What expenses?" I asked. "All we need are the tickets."

My mom smiled at me as if I wasn't capable of understanding the most basic thing. "You've got to think about the travel costs," she said. "You girls are asking to stay in a hotel or rent a condo, neither of which is free. Plus, there's gas and food to worry about."

"We can bring our own food—peanut-butter-and-jelly sandwiches all around! Plus, I'll fill up my camp canteen with water so you don't even have to spring for a soda. It'll be great *and* healthy."

Ted nodded as if considering this. "That's an interesting idea, but things still add up, sweetie."

"What if we subsist on peanut butter alone?" I asked. "Forget the jelly!"

My mom and Ted laughed, even though I was being serious. "I'm talking not even bread. We'll bring our own spoons and eat straight from the jar."

"We don't expect you to pay for everything," said my mom. "But we decided fifty dollars was fair."

"Fifty dollars each?" I asked. "Okay, I guess that's fair."

"No, fifty dollars per kid for the food and travel," my mom said. "The ticket doesn't count. You're looking at one hundred and fifty dollars total per kid, and there are five of you so that's—"

"That's seven hundred and fifty dollars!" I shouted, horrified by the prospect.

"Very nice math skills," Ted said, offering me a high five.

I left him high and dry because I wasn't in the mood. "That's not the point!" I said. "Seven hundred and fifty dollars is a fortune!"

"We'll cover the rest," my mom said. "Tickets for two chaperones and whatever you girls spend beyond that. You're really getting off easy, if you think about it, because the weekend will probably cost about twice as much as that."

"At least," Ted added.

I looked back and forth suspiciously between my mom and Ted. "Whose idea was this anyway? Not yours, I hope."

My mom smiled. "All of us parents got together and came up with this solution. We also agreed not to name names. It doesn't matter who had the idea because we all think it's a wonderful plan."

"You do realize that we're in the sixth grade, right? And that none of us has actually had a paying job before. Probably because, technically, it's illegal for children to work in this country."

I took a bite of my pancakes. They were delicious, but I wasn't going to say so out loud. Not with the kind of news they'd just dropped on me.

My mom sighed and said, "The concert sounds like a lot of fun. But it's also expensive fun. You girls are old enough to appreciate that, and we think you're old enough to figure out how to make it work."

"Plus, you'll appreciate the music more if you work hard to earn the money for the tickets," said Ted.

I gulped down my last bite of breakfast. "All our favorite bands are playing—we will appreciate it no matter what!"

"I know this seems like a crazy thing, but trust us," said Ted. "We know what we're doing."

I narrowed my eyes at Ted, because if this whole crazy plan was his idea, well, that seemed way unfair. My mom has been my mom ever since I was born. Meanwhile, Ted has only been my stepfather since December. His opinion shouldn't matter that much!

I didn't say any of this out loud because I didn't want to hurt anyone's feelings, but my mom must've read my mind. "As I mentioned before," she said, "all of your friends' parents and I agreed we weren't going to name names."

"So this is basically one gigantic conspiracy," I argued. "Which is sad, because the concert money is going toward such a good cause. Don't you care about the pandas?"

"Of course we do," said my mom.

"Don't stress about this, Annabelle. You're smart and so are your friends," said Ted. "You'll figure out a way to come up with the money."

There was no getting through to them, so I cleared my plate and grabbed my backpack.

"Oh, before I forget," my mom said, "want to come shopping with me after school on Friday?"

"Totally!" I said. "There's this new jean jacket I've been wanting."

My mom laughed. "Okay, we'll see if we have time for that, but I have a bunch of shopping to do for the baby and I thought you'd want to come."

I shrugged. "Sure, why not?"

"Great." My mom smiled. "It'll be fun. I'm taking the afternoon off, so I'll pick you up after school."

"Sounds good," I said. "See ya later."

It wasn't until lunchtime that my friends and I were finally all together so we could discuss this debacle.

"I cannot believe they're doing this to us!" Claire cried, burying her face in her hands. "We're only twelve years old. How are we supposed to come up with seven hundred and fifty dollars?"

"They may as well ask us to earn a billion dollars," I said. "And I'm only eleven."

"See," Claire announced, even though everyone at our table was privy to the same conversation. "It's worse than I thought. Annabelle is only eleven."

"Wait, are the rest of you twelve already?" I asked. I looked to all my friends, who nodded. Yes, they were all twelve. "I can't believe I'm the shortest one and the youngest one in the group!"

"Believe it," said Yumi. "But you're almost twelve, right?"

I nodded. "My birthday is in three more weeks."

"What are you doing for your birthday?" Rachel asked. "Are you going to rent a limo? I heard Nikki rented a limo for all her friends and they went to the mall to get makeovers and then they went to Malibu to have seafood at this super-fancy place on the beach. She made all her friends wear dresses or skirts. No pants allowed!"

"That's totally weird," said Claire, shuddering. "A dress code for a birthday party is insane, and yet, so totally Nikki."

"Why would I do any of that?" I asked, feeling that same sense of uneasiness from the sleepover in the pit of my stomach.

Rachel shrugged and turned back to her peanut-butter-and-banana sandwich, taking a large bite and chewing. Like having a mouth full of food was an excuse not to explain herself. Except it wasn't. But did I even need her explanation when I kind of knew what she was getting at?

"Are you asking me if I'm going to have the same party as Nikki because we both live in Canyon Ranch?" I asked pointedly.

Rachel gave an exaggerated shrug. "You said it. Not me."

Emma cleared her throat and said, "I have lived in Canyon Ranch since I was born and I've never even been in a limo."

"Thank you," I said.

"Now, let's get back to the concert money," Emma said as she pulled out a notebook and pen and made some calculations. "I'm just saying it's not as impossible as it sounds. Think about it. There are five of us. Today is April fifteenth, and the concert isn't until July fourth. That's almost three months away. We've got plenty of time to figure out how to raise the money."

"It's a lot of money. At least for me," Rachel said, staring at me.

"It's a lot for all of us," I said.

Claire nodded and pulled out her phone to use the calculator. "But Emma is right. When you break it down, you can see we have to come up with two hundred and fifty dollars a month. That's about fifty-six dollars a week, or eight dollars a day. Divide that by five, and each of us has to raise less than two dollars a day."

"Totally manageable!" said Emma.

"But that's if you include today. If we start tomorrow, we're already behind," said Rachel.

"Not necessarily," said Emma. "Let's start by pooling what we have so far."

"Good idea. Who has money?" asked Claire, looking around the table. "I have twenty dollars left over from what my grandma gave me for Easter."

"You get money for Easter?" asked Rachel.

"Only this year because my grandma felt guilty for celebrating with her boyfriend's family instead of us."

"I counted my savings after my dad broke the

news to me last night," said Yumi. "I have eighteen dollars and seventy-five cents, mostly from babysitting for my little sister."

I scratched my head and thought for a moment. "I haven't counted my money in a while, and I'm not even sure where my piggy bank is, but I think I have something like six dollars, plus a jar of pennies."

My friends nodded, none of them very impressed.

"The jar is pretty big," I felt the need to add. "There's probably at least three dollars in there. I'll count it when I get home from school."

"Perfect," said Emma. "If we assume your estimation is correct, that's nine dollars. And adding that to Yumi's and Claire's money, it means we have forty-seven dollars and seventy-five cents."

"I have thirty dollars, plus I got a quarter as change when I bought my lunch. So that makes seventy-eight dollars." Emma turned to Rachel. "See! We're actually way ahead of the game."

"Yeah," said Claire. "What do you have?"

Rachel shook her head. "I'm totally broke. I only get seven dollars a week for my allowance, and I already spent this week's money on frozen yogurt."

My ears perked up. Rachel got seven dollars a week for an allowance? That was a big allowance as far as I was concerned and I decided to tell her so.

'That's a lot of money," I said.

"It's only a dollar a day," said Rachel. "You can't buy anything for a dollar."

"I don't even get an allowance," I said.

"You don't?" asked Emma.

"Nope." I shook my head. "My mom says I have to help out around the house because it's my house too. I shouldn't be rewarded for making my bed or doing my dishes, for instance. It's my bed and my dishes and part of the garbage is mine too. When my mom asks me to do something, I'm supposed to do it."

"So what happens when you need to buy something?" asked Claire.

"Well, I just ask," I said with a shrug. "If I want to go to a movie or I want a new outfit or something, I'll tell my mom, and if she has the money, she'll give it to me. And if not, she'll tell me. Or she'll say that whatever jeans I want are too expensive and I can get a less-fancy pair or we can wait until the ones I want are on sale."

"Well, whenever I want to go to a movie, I have to use my own money," said Rachel.

"But you always get money, every single week no matter what," I pointed out. "Which means you could see two movies every month if you wanted to—and buy popcorn."

"As long as I do my chores," said Rachel. "It's not like I can just ask."

"I told you it's not that easy," I said. "I don't always get what I want."

Rachel frowned as if she didn't believe me.

"Let's get back to the concert," said Emma. "Right now we've got seventy-eight dollars."

"Which means we don't even have enough money for one ticket," said Rachel.

"True," said Emma. "But we do have plenty of cash to start a business with." She turned to Yumi and asked, "You said you've been earning money babysitting?"

"Yup," said Yumi. "I'm in charge of my baby sister every single night for twenty minutes while my mom makes dinner."

"How much do you make?" I asked.

"Five dollars an hour," said Yumi. "So that works out to be eleven dollars and change every week."

"You are so lucky," said Claire. "Maybe we can all babysit for Suki."

Emma scratched some numbers into her notebook. "We'd have to babysit for one hundred and fifty hours to make enough money."

"We do have three whole months," Yumi pointed out.

"Yeah, but do you think your parents need that much help?" I asked.

Yumi thought about this for a minute. "Well, Suki has another babysitter. I'm more of a mother's helper, which means I watch her when my parents are in the house but busy with something. They say I can't babysit for real until I'm fourteen."

"Too bad," said Emma.

"Yeah," said Yumi. "Anyway, I don't think she'd pay all five of us to watch Suki at the same time."

"Okay, so much for babysitting," said Emma, crossing it off her list.

"Wait, I know a five-year-old named Sienna," said Rachel. "She moved into Annabelle's old house and her mom also has a baby. Maybe I could be a mother's helper."

"Good idea," said Emma. "Definitely look into that and report back. And in the meantime let's think of some sort of business we could run."

"Why don't we set up a lemonade stand?" Claire suggested. "It's perfect now that the weather is warming up. Who doesn't love lemonade?"

I looked around at my friends. The smiles on our faces told me that we all loved lemonade.

"I sold lemonade on my corner last Fourth of July and I totally cleaned up!" Rachel said.

"I know, I was there," said Claire. "And how fun was it?"

"It was the best," said Rachel as they high-fived each other.

"How soon can we get started?" I asked.

"Well, we need lemonade and a stand," said Emma. "And we probably have to do some sort of advertising so people actually know we have a stand."

"And we have to figure out where to set it up," said Yumi.

"Wherever there are thirsty people," Rachel said.

"And wherever it's super-hot," I said. "Good news— I've been checking the weather constantly ever since we moved. Saturday is definitely swim weather. Which means it'll be lemonade weather too. How about we meet after school at my house. We can figure everything out."

"Done!" said Claire. "This is going to be awesome!"

"Is everyone else in?" I asked.

My friends nodded. Even Rachel.

The bell rang. We all high-fived and then cleaned up our lunches and went to class.

I had science with Tobias and Oliver.

As soon as I sat down, Oliver smiled at me and said, "You're in a good mood. Fun lunch?"

"It's got nothing to do with lunch," I said. "I'm just excited because my friends and I figured out how to get to the Panda Parade."

"The what?" asked Tobias.

"The Panda Parade. It's this big concert that's happening in Indio in July."

"My grandparents live in Indio," said Tobias, brushing his greasy black hair out of his eyes. "It's so boring there. It's all flat and hot, and there's nothing but desert and mini-malls as far as the eye can see."

"Well, it won't be boring when I'm there for Fourth of July weekend, because the Panda Parade is going to be amazing."

"Again, the what?" asked Tobias.

I told them all about the concert.

"I'm allergic to pandas," said Tobias.

"There aren't actually going to be pandas there," I told him. "That's the problem. The pandas are endangered, meaning they're not enough of them in the world. So all my favorite bands are getting together to throw a benefit concert in Indio."

"Sounds fun," said Oliver, tossing his pen in the air and catching it again. "I should go."

"You should!" I said.

"Except I don't know what my plans are for the summer," said Oliver. "I need to check with my mom. We may not be around."

"Wait, what do you mean?" I asked. "Where are you going?"

"We usually go to Europe so I can visit my grandparents."

Oliver's mom is from Jamaica and his dad is from England. It made sense that he had family in other countries. It just never occurred to me that he'd be leaving mine!

"No way! For how long?"

"The summer," said Oliver.

"The entire summer?"

Oliver shrugged. "I think so. A month or so, anyway."

"That's so long!" I said without thinking about the fact that Tobias was listening to every single word we said.

"Aw, poor Oliver and Annabelle," he teased. "The lovebirds are going to be torn apart. . . . How will you two survive?"

I was about to tell Tobias to shut his mouth, but Oliver did before I had the chance to.

"We mean it!" I said, socking him on the shoulder for good measure.

"Ouch! You two are the worst lab partners ever," said Tobias, slumping in his chair and crossing his arms over his chest. His dark hair hung over his eyes, but this time he didn't bother pushing it back. "I'm totally outnumbered."

I had to laugh because I had felt the exact same way at the beginning of the school year when Tobias and Oliver were all buddy-buddy and I was the new kid. I suppose my experience could have given me some extra sympathy for Tobias. Except I couldn't forget the way he had tortured me earlier this school year—kicking my chair and calling me Spazabelle and even stealing my homework once. So it was hard to feel bad for the dude.

"Deal with it," I said.

"You are harsh," he replied.

I simply smiled at him and said, "I kind of have to be to deal with you."

"Nice one," Oliver whispered.

I grinned and nodded and said, "Yeah, I try."

chapter five
the perfect plan

Some days I wish I had a gigantic fast-forward button for my life, because whenever I'm excited about doing something after school, classes seem to move super-slowly. It's like the universe knew I had big plans and it was making my teachers even more boring than usual. And this particular afternoon seemed worse than ever.

When the dismissal bell finally rang, I scrambled to my locker to meet up with my four best friends. We gathered all our things and made sure we had the right books for our homework (because we're nerdy like that), and then we walked to my place.

My mom and Ted were still at work, so I let everyone inside with my key, which I kept clipped to a special hook inside my backpack so it didn't get lost.

Pepper barked and jumped on me right away, as usual. I led him to the backyard so Rachel wouldn't start sneezing.

"Anyone want a snack?" I asked after making sure the back door was firmly closed. "We have carrots and cheese sticks and oatmeal-chocolate-chip cookies. . . ."

"Cookies!" Claire and Emma said at the same time, and the rest of us laughed.

"Yeah, why'd I even ask about the healthy stuff?" I wondered out loud as I headed for the kitchen.

Everyone else filed into the living room and sat down on our new white sofa. That made me realize something. I wasn't sure if we were allowed to eat in the living room. My mom and Ted had never said not to, but then again, I'd never seen them take food in there before.

I figured it would be okay, but I still felt like I should be responsible and say something. So when I brought the plate of cookies over and set them down on the coffee table, I said, "Careful with the food in the living room, okay, guys? Everything is new."

Most of my friends nodded. Claire said, "Of course."

But Rachel rolled her eyes and said, "Don't worry, Annabelle. We'll be careful in your fancy living room."

"That's not what I meant," I said, arranging the napkins next to the plate. "It's just, I know my mom and Ted would get upset if the couch got stained. There's nothing wrong with that. Right? I mean, Emma we're not allowed to eat in your living room."

"True," said Emma.

"Mine, either," said Yumi. "My parents don't even let people wear shoes in the house."

"See," I said to Rachel. I know I sounded defensive, but I guess that made sense since I *was* defending myself. The thing was, I didn't know why I had to. I didn't want to have to.

"Whatever," said Rachel, acting all pouty. "You don't have to jump down my throat."

"You're the one who started this," I said.

"No, you're the one who can't stop talking about her fabulous new life in Canyon Ranch," Rachel said.

Claire gasped, and Emma's and Yumi's eyes got wide. As for me? I felt as if I'd been punched in the stomach. My eyes got teary, and I blinked hard and took a deep breath, trying to figure out what to say.

"I don't know where these comments are coming from, Rachel. But my life is exactly the same as it ever was. We simply moved to a new house."

"Which you can't stop talking about," said Rachel.

Claire looked back and forth between us nervously. "Let's just agree to disagree. Okay, guys?" she said.

"What are we even disagreeing about?" asked Rachel. "I am always careful when I eat. And who's the one who spilled orange juice all over the dining room table at my place last month?"

"That's because your brother threw a basketball at my head!" I said. "And you promised me it wasn't a big deal."

"It wasn't," said Rachel. "Spills happen everywhere. But stop making Jackson out to be some monster. It was a Nerf basketball, and he yelled 'catch' before he threw it."

"Technically, he yelled catch after it bounced off my face," I said. "But more important—I can't believe you're taking your brother's side on this one."

"I'm not. I'm simply stating some facts," said Rachel, crossing her arms over her chest and leaning back on the couch.

"Know what? Let's go eat in the kitchen," said Emma, grabbing the plate of cookies as she stood up. "It'll be much easier."

Everyone else followed her, and we sat down at the table. Then Emma pulled her notebook out of her backpack. "Let's get started. First let's make a list of supplies."

"For a lemonade stand?" asked Rachel. "We should probably start with some lemonade. Right, guys?"

She looked at all of us around the table, probably expecting some laughs, but no one gave her any and I refused to meet her gaze. I was still so annoyed about her comments. They totally ruined what was supposed to be a fun afternoon.

"Sure, that's obvious," said Claire. "But do we make our own or buy it from the store or buy a mix and make it from that?"

"Let's make our own from scratch," said Emma. "Freshly squeezed lemonade always tastes better than the store-bought kind."

"It's cheaper, too," said Claire.

"Right." Emma nodded and wrote down 'lemonade from scratch' in her notebook. "It sounds more special that way too. Like anyone can go out and *buy* lemonade, but to actually make it by hand?"

"Yeah, so we need lemons, water, and sugar. Unless we want to make strawberry lemonade or something," said Claire.

"Or mint lemonade," I added. "I had that last week when I went out to dinner with my mom, and it was delicious."

"Oh, that sounds fancy," Rachel said.

I stole a quick glance at Rachel and tried to figure out if she was being positive or critical about my suggestion. I hated that it was so hard to tell these days. But I decided to give her the benefit of the doubt. "It was fancy!" I said brightly.

Luckily, she didn't make a rude remark—this time!

"I love mint lemonade," said Claire. "Have you guys been to the restaurant called Lemonade? They always have six different flavors on hand."

"Six?" asked Rachel.

"Yup," said Claire. "Last week they had blueberry lemonade, and strawberry, mint, and even kale lemonade."

"Kale lemonade sounds disgusting!" Rachel said.

"It kind of is," said Claire. "But people must buy it or they wouldn't sell it, right?"

"Can we sell sparkling lemonade?" asked Yumi. "That's my favorite kind and it's so easy to make. All you do is add seltzer to it."

Emma thought about this for a few moments and frowned. "Having a bunch of different kinds of lemonade is a good idea in theory, but I think it'll be too complicated in the execution."

"What if we only make two or three kinds?" asked Claire.

"That makes sense," said Emma. "But let's get the basics down first. Like, for the first week is it okay if we focus on straight-up, old-fashioned plain lemonade?"

"Sounds good to me," I said.

"Good. Does anyone here have a lemon tree in their backyard?" Emma asked, looking around.

"I do," I said, raising my hand.

"So do I," Emma and Rachel said at the same time.

"We have two lemon trees, but they're in our front yard," said Yumi.

"That'll work too!" said Claire. "Everyone can pick their own lemons. Our parents can't object to that since we're picking them for a good cause."

"This is all for the pandas!" Yumi yelled, pumping one fist in the air.

"And our own enjoyment!" Rachel added.

"You mean our musical education," Emma said.

"Yes, that sounds so much better," I said.

"We need cups, too," said Emma. "And pitchers to put the lemonade in, and sugar, unless we want to go with another sweetener."

"Like honey," said Claire. "Or agave. My moms are way into agave these days."

"I've never even heard of agave," said Rachel, wrinkling her nose.

"It's sweeter than refined sugar and way better for you," said Claire. "I'll bring some. We probably don't even need to buy it because we have a huge bottle from Costco and a little bit goes a long way."

"If *I'd* mentioned agave, you probably would have said it was too fancy," I mumbled under my breath.

"What?" asked Rachel.

"Nothing," I said.

Claire, who was sitting right next to me, definitely heard what I said but decided not to comment on it. "We'll also need ice," she said instead, shooting me a glance as if to warn me not to pick a fight. "It's going to be hot out."

"Can everyone bring ice from their freezers?" asked Rachel.

Everyone nodded and Emma checked ice off her list. "We are in amazing shape." She looked up from her notebook. "Now, does anyone have a wagon so we can transport all our supplies?"

"Oh, my baby sister does," said Yumi. "And she

can't object to us borrowing it because she doesn't know how to talk yet."

"Perfect!" said Rachel, clapping her hands.

"And Ted has a giant cooler. It's even on wheels," I said.

"Good. Now what we need is a cool name for the stand. Oh, and the actual stand. I can design that," said Claire. "My parents won't mind if I use their poker table and I was thinking about tie-dyeing a sheet and then writing on it with some puffy paint. Then we just need something to frame it with. I have an old puppet-show stand that'll probably work."

"Why tie-dye?" asked Rachel.

"So it'll stand out," said Claire. "I say the brighter colors, the better."

"That's kind of your motto in life," I said.

Claire looked down at herself—she happened to be wearing a red-purple-and-turquoise shirt that was half striped and half polka dots. Her faded blue jeans had yellow bandanna patches on the knees. Also, she had on red flip-flops, and each of her toenails was painted a different color of the rainbow. It all sounded kind of scrappy, I realized, but on Claire it totally worked. And she knew it!

"It's been working out well for me so far," she said.

"It's an interesting advertising strategy," said Emma, nodding thoughtfully. "Certainly, eye-catching is good." She took some more notes.

"What do you keep writing down?" asked Claire,

looking over Emma's shoulder. "A profit and loss statement? Are you putting together an entire business plan?"

"Of course," said Emma. She tucked her hair behind her ears and gave a closed-mouth grin.

"Is that necessary?" asked Claire. "Kids have been making lemonade stands for centuries."

"And we want to make sure ours is the best," said Emma. "That means we've got to think about branding. People need to know that our lemonade stands for something: quality and great taste, freshness, and general deliciousness."

"So what do we call the stand so it conveys all those messages?" Claire wondered.

"'Please buy some lemonade so we can go to a concert,'" said Yumi.

"No, make it about the pandas," said Emma. "If people think they're contributing to a good cause— and they are, indirectly—they'll be more likely to spend money."

"'Lemonade for Pandas,'" said Claire.

"Oh, I like it!" I said.

"It's simple and to the point," Emma agreed.

"Yeah—it's perfect," said Yumi.

"Lemonade for Pandas it is," Rachel agreed.

"So where should we set up our storefront?" asked Emma. "Or our stand-front, I suppose I should call it."

"How about right here in Canyon Ranch?" asked

Rachel. "This is where all the rich people live. They've got lots of extra money to spend for the pandas, I'll bet."

"There are plenty of normal people in Canyon Ranch," I argued.

"Sorry, didn't mean to offend you," said Rachel.

"I'm not offended because I'm not rich," I said.

"How come saying you're rich is offensive?" asked Rachel. "I wish I were rich."

"Look, none of us is exactly starving," Claire pointed out. "We all have nice places to live and cute clothes and plenty of food to eat."

"But some people have bigger houses than others," Rachel said. "And more clothes, too."

"Why are you so obsessed with pointing that out all of the sudden?" asked Claire.

"I'm not obsessed," said Rachel.

"You kind of are," said Yumi.

"How come you're all picking on me?" Rachel cried.

"Can we please stop talking about money?" said Emma. "And start working on actually making some? Rachel, back to your point about having the lemonade stand in this neighborhood: I actually don't think it's the best idea because there's hardly any foot traffic on these streets. We need to be somewhere more public."

"Like the mall," said Claire. "Except we can't sell anything at the mall without a permit. I know, because my brother tried to sell his old baseball cards there last year and someone called the police on him."

"Did he get arrested?" I asked.

"No, some security guard came over and made him stop. But even though he got off with a warning, it was still plenty scary."

"Why don't we set up near the playground?" I said. "It's baseball season and there are tons of games on Saturday. Oliver's team is playing. . . ."

"Wait, are you trying to use our lemonade stand as an excuse to see your boyfriend?" asked Rachel.

"I don't need an excuse to see my boyfriend," I reminded her. "He only lives eight houses away."

Rachel rolled her eyes. "As you keep reminding us. We all know you live in Canyon Ranch now, Annabelle. Don't worry—we won't forget."

"I didn't even mention Canyon Ranch."

Emma held out her hands and said, "Stop fighting, guys."

"We're not fighting," I said. "I'm only stating some facts."

"As am I," Rachel said in the prissiest tone I'd ever heard.

I glanced at my watch, wishing all my friends would go home. It was a pretty lousy sentiment, I realized, but I couldn't help myself. This whole day was turning out to be rotten, thanks to Rachel. Whenever she opened her mouth, I automatically felt defensive and on edge. I couldn't help it. And it wasn't just that Rachel was in a grumpy mood, because she was fine with everyone else. Rachel had been acting mad at me for days—ever since I moved to Canyon Ranch.

"So are we set?" I asked.

"Yes," said Emma, closing her notebook. "We have all week to get ready and it looks like we are, as long as someone has plastic cups."

"We've got tons of plastic cups," said Claire.

"Perfect," said Emma. "I should get going now. I have a ton of homework."

"Me too," said Yumi and Claire at the same time.

Rachel didn't say anything. She just followed my friends to the front door. It may have been my imagination, but it seemed like everyone wanted to leave. And I didn't blame them!

We went to Emma's house after school on Tuesday so we could perfect our recipe. Turns out we needed about three times as much water as lemon juice, plus three squirts of agave nectar to get the perfect batch.

Then on Thursday we went to Claire's place to work on the actual stand. She'd tie-dyed a sheet ahead of time and it was amazing—color bursts of rainbow with the words LEMONADE FOR PANDAS spelled out in silver glitter paint.

By the end of that day we were raring to go. We thought the lemonade stand was going to be awesome, and the answer to all our financial concerns.

We figured we'd make what we needed for the concert and would have plenty of money left over, too.

Except the lemonade stand was a disaster of epic proportions—the worst thing to happen to our friendship.

And I wasn't even sure how things got so bad.

chapter six
when life gives you lemons, do not make lemonade

The trouble started at lunch on Friday, the day before our grand opening. And surprisingly, it had nothing to do with lemonade.

"I was thinking of whipping up a batch of my famous chocolate-chip-banana mini-muffins for tomorrow's lemonade stand," Claire said.

It seemed like an innocent statement to me, but Emma jumped down her throat, as if Claire had suggested digging for oil in our backyards—with our bare hands.

"Muffins?" she practically shouted as she literally dropped her tuna fish sandwich on the table. "Why would we sell muffins?"

"Because they're delicious," said Claire. "And anyway, who doesn't love a mini-muffin to go with their lemonade?"

I was about to tell her it was a great idea, but before I had the chance to, Emma cut in. And her voice sounded way high-pitched. Also? She talked faster than usual, as if she were nervous or angry but trying to hide it.

"Introducing two new products at once could be confusing," said Emma. "I feel like it's smarter to focus on one thing—at least for our opening weekend. You know, like we all agreed to the other day. I've been reading up a lot about how to launch a new business, and everyone seems to agree that it's best to start simple and really perfect the basics."

"Emma's right. And we did agree to serve plain lemonade before even trying out other flavors," Yumi gently reminded Claire.

"How come you always take Emma's side?" Claire asked her.

"I don't, and I'm not even taking sides," said Yumi, sitting up straighter. "I'm merely offering my opinion about what products we should be selling."

"You sound just like Emma now!" Claire said.

"What's that supposed to mean?" Yumi asked, clearly offended.

"You don't have to be so formal and official about it," said Claire. "Muffins aren't a product. They're just muffins."

"Think about the size of the table," said Emma. "And how crowded it would be with more than one thing on it."

"I think the table can handle two things," said Claire with a laugh.

Emma shook her head. "But its not simply two things. We've got the pitcher of lemonade and the cups and the ice and the cash box."

"The ice is going to go in the cooler on the ground," said Claire.

"True, but there's got to be room for us, too," Yumi pointed out. "Your moms' poker table isn't that big."

"I can fit a dozen miniature muffins on one small plate," said Claire. "I've done it before."

"I love mini-muffins," said Rachel.

"Me too," I said. "And you know what's also delicious? Muffin tops."

"Last year my aunt bought me a muffin top muffin tin for my birthday," said Rachel. "Except I've been using it to make cupcake tops instead. So what if we did that with the frosting on top? I mean, how awesome would that be?"

"Or what about cake pops?" asked Claire. "They hardly take up any space because they're the size of lollipops. I think you can even buy a cake-pop holder. This keeps getting better and better."

"Or at least sweeter and sweeter," I said. "The other day I went out to this bakery with my mom and Ted. My mom has a huge sweet tooth now, thanks to the pregnancy, which I'm totally benefiting from. Anyway, they sold frosting shots."

"What's that, like a bullet made out of frosting?"

asked Claire. "Do you shoot it out of a gun made of cake?"

"No, no, no," I said. "It's in a little shot glass. Like how grownups can order a shot of espresso, or cowboys order shots of whiskey in those tiny little glasses? This is the frosting version."

"You mean you can get all the frosting without having to bother with the cake part? That sounds amazing," said Claire, her eyes getting way wide. "We've got to sell frosting shots. That's way better than mini-muffins. Awesome idea, Annabelle!"

Emma looked at Yumi, who rolled her eyes.

"What?" Claire asked Emma.

"Nothing," said Emma.

"No, I saw you roll your eyes just now, and you and Yumi gave each other that look."

"What look?" asked Yumi.

"You know!" said Claire.

Yumi shook her head. "I have no idea what you're talking about."

Emma turned to me. "Frosting shots sound good, but on Monday we all agreed to lemonade, and I think we should stick to it."

"I'm not saying we shouldn't sell lemonade," said Claire. "I'm just saying we should also sell frosting shots. I mean, think about it—lemonade stands are as old as time. But lemonade-and-frosting-shot stands? We might very well be the first ever!"

"What if we combine the two and sell lemonade-flavored frosting shots?" asked Rachel.

"And lemonade, too?" asked Claire. "Or just the frosting shots?"

"Good question," said Rachel. "What do you think, Emma?"

Emma gave the rest of us a pained expression. "I think we should stick to the original plan."

"Mini-muffins?" asked Claire.

"No, lemonade!" Emma shouted.

"You don't have to yell," said Claire. "I'm sitting right across the table."

"I know, but I'm frustrated because you can't just change your mind!"

"Of course I can," said Claire. "People change their minds all the time. It's not good to be so rigid."

"Gah!" Emma buried her head in her hands.

"Now you've got this sour-lemon expression on your face," said Claire.

"I do not," said Emma, glaring at Claire.

I didn't want to get in the middle of things, but Claire was right. Emma totally looked like she was sucking on lemon slices. And I kind of understood why. She'd worked hard on the business plan and had a good reason to want to stick to the lemonade. On the other hand, it was hard to beat Claire's enthusiasm. And mini-muffins did sound delicious.

"Let's just try selling the muffins," said Claire. "I really don't think it has to be a big deal. A lemonade–

bake sale will only bring in more money for our concert tickets, which is what this is all about. Right?"

"Well, what about the sign?" asked Emma. "You already made it, and there's no room to add anything about muffins."

"Maybe we don't have to advertise it," said Claire. "Maybe the muffins will come as a nice surprise."

"If we sell muffins, I think we need to advertise the muffins," said Emma. "That's, like, the most basic thing in the world."

Claire thought about this for a moment as she pulled her hair into a bun. "I can scrunch in a '+muffins' right next to the lemonade. I've got some spare puffy paint at my house."

"Does that mean that you'll provide muffins whenever we have lemonade?" asked Emma. "And if so, who's going to pay for the supplies?"

"I don't know," said Claire. "But I'm sure we'll figure it out. What's the big deal?"

"This is a huge deal! What if we spend too much money and don't make enough for tickets?" asked Emma.

"Hey, let's vote on it," suggested Rachel.

"Good idea," said Claire. "I mean, no one made you the boss, right, Emma?"

Emma sucked in her breath, shocked. "I never said I was the boss."

"Good," said Claire. "I'm glad to see this is still a democracy. Let's vote!"

I didn't want to take sides, but I could already tell who stood where. Yumi and Emma seemed in agreement. So did Rachel and Claire. As for me, well, I saw both sides. Mini-muffins sounded delicious and like a good way to earn some extra money. But at the same time—Emma had made some valid points. Our table was small, and the sign was already done. Plus, maybe we should keep things as simple as possible for the opening week.

I didn't know which side to take, but I knew I'd be the deciding vote. It was a lot of pressure.

"Everyone who wants muffins, raise your hand," said Claire. She held her hand up high and Rachel did too.

"And everyone who doesn't want muffins at our Lemonade for Pandas stand, raise your hand," said Emma, smiling, assuming that the majority of us was anti-muffin.

She and Yumi both raised their hands.

Then everyone turned to me.

"I abstain," I said, sitting on my hands.

"You can't abstain," said Emma. "We need you to decide."

"It's too much pressure!" I said. "Let's flip a coin."

Everyone sighed as I pulled a quarter out of my pocket.

"Hey, is that a new jacket?" asked Rachel.

I looked down at my jacket. "It is," I said. "My mom got it for me last night."

"But you already had a jean jacket," Rachel said, kind of pointedly. Almost like she was complaining.

"I know," I said, feeling uneasy. "But this one has a dark wash and the other was all faded."

"Huh," said Rachel.

She didn't say anything else, but she didn't have to. That single syllable said so much: Rachel was jealous of my jean jacket. Or maybe Rachel was jealous of me in general. Or maybe Rachel was just highly critical of everything I did or said or wore these days. Why was she keeping track of how many jackets I had? What was wrong with getting a new jacket? Nothing!

"People get new jackets sometimes. There's no need to comment on it," I said to Rachel, flipping my hair over my shoulder. I felt kind of mean saying it, and I'm not sure why since I was merely stating a fact.

Rachel smirked and said, "Some people get more jackets than—"

"Hey," said Yumi, interrupting. "Let's drop it. We need to make a call on the banana muffins."

Everyone turned to me in anticipation.

"Know what," I said. "Let's not flip a coin. I changed my mind. Let's sell lemonade this weekend and really make the stand great. Maybe we can try muffins the following week. As long as everything else is under control."

"There you go," said Emma. "It's settled."

Claire huffed and rolled her eyes.

Rachel stared at me, her head tilted, as if she were trying to figure something out. Like maybe I had voted not only against muffins but against her.

I could tell that was what she suspected, and it annoyed me even more.

Because guess what? Rachel was totally right.

chapter seven
shop till you drop . . .
a huge wad of cash!

My mom picked me up from school later that day, and we headed straight for the mini-mall. I don't even know how many times I'd passed by the Baby Supply Company on my way to the Gap, but I'd never actually been inside. I'd never had any reason to go until now.

That was why it was such a shock to see how massive the place was. Walking inside, I felt like I was in an airplane hangar. Except instead of planes, it was filled with enough supplies to take care of a gazillion babies. The ceilings were so high, and the walls were all lined with shelves stacked higher than any regular-size human could reach. From where we stood, right inside the front doors, I couldn't even see the end of the store.

"This place is crazy!" I said to my mom.

"I know." She laughed. "It's pastels and plastics as far as the eye can see. Who knew there was so much stuff they could sell to new parents?"

"Not me," I said as we walked through an entire

aisle dedicated to high chairs and stopped when we got to the parking-lot-size space for strollers. "Some of these look more like rocket ships," I said.

My mom tested one out—pushing it back and forth. "Yeah, they didn't have ones so elaborate when you were little. At least I don't think they did. I bought your stroller used off Craigslist. It's all so different this time around."

"You mean because you have Ted?" I asked carefully.

When I was born, my mom was on her own. By the time she realized she was pregnant with me, she'd already broken up with my biological dad, and he didn't want to have anything to do with me. He still doesn't, not that I care. He lives in Norway, which is in Scandinavia, which is really, really, really far from here.

"Yes," said my mom. "It's nice knowing I'm not going to have to go through everything alone. Although I wouldn't change a thing about raising you." She put her arm around my shoulders and kissed me on the top of my head. "And I'm thrilled to know I can do it on my own if I have to. Nothing will ever be that intimidating."

I stared at my mom. She looked massive in her giant sundress with red and blue sideways stripes. Her feet were swollen and she had on purple flip-flops. They were the only shoes she could wear now—I'd heard her complain to Ted that her feet were too big for all her regular shoes. She didn't even walk anymore.

She waddled, which looked weird and funny, but I didn't want to say so because I figured that would be insulting.

Anyway, as we walked she continued adding stuff to the shopping cart. Baby towels with yellow ducks all over them, little jumper things with bunnies and rainbows, a white plastic bathtub with blue padding, and two gigantic boxes of newborn-size diapers.

"Wow, those should last for a year!" I said.

My mom laughed. "More like a month if we're lucky!"

We wandered through the crib section and found dozens on display—all in different shapes and sizes and colors and designs. And there were pictures of a hundred more in a gigantic binder with big laminated pictures.

Except the one crib that my mom wanted wasn't in stock.

She asked the salesperson—a tall guy with curly, salt-and-pepper hair—about the crib.

He plugged some numbers into his computer and said, "That one's on back order and won't be ready to ship for another three weeks, ma'am."

"Are you sure about that?" asked my mom, holding on to her belly with both hands as if she were holding the baby in place. "Because we can't wait much longer."

"Positive," he replied with a curt nod.

"Okay, then," said my mom. She gave the sales

83

guy our address and he handed her a piece of paper with a picture of the crib on it.

"They'll ring it up at the register with the rest of your stuff," he explained. "Just give them your address and the crib will be delivered straight to you."

"Thank you," she said as we turned the corner and headed to yet another section of the store.

"Don't worry, Annabelle. We're almost done here," she said as if reading my mind. "Want to help me pick out sheets?"

"Sure," I said, pointing to the first set I saw and liked. "How about those with the blue and yellow elephants?"

"Lovely," said my mom. "And they're organic, too." She took three sets and dropped them into her cart. Then she pushed the cart toward the cash register. Since she seemed to be struggling, I asked if she wanted me to take over.

"That would be amazing," she said.

I got behind the cart and tried to push it, but it didn't move. "Wow, this is heavy," I said, throwing more weight behind my steps.

"I don't know what I'd do without you," my mom said. She shuffled along, tummy out, her hands resting on her back.

"Why, where am I going?" I asked. "Do you plan on sending me to boarding school once this kid comes out?"

My mom cracked up. "No, you're not going anywhere. This baby is going to need you."

"Good," I said as we joined the back of the line. I looked at the sheets again, hoping my baby brother or sister would like them. Being a big sister suddenly felt like a huge responsibility, and I hoped I was good at it.

"Did you know that Yumi is in charge of her baby sister, Suki, every night when her mom makes dinner?" I asked.

"I didn't," my mom said, smiling.

"She even gets paid for it," I said.

"Good for her," my mom said.

There were only two carts in front of us, but both of them were stuffed full of baby junk too, so we ended up having to wait for a while.

When our checkout time finally came, it took forever for the cashier to ring up all the items, and once she finished, well, I could not believe the bill. I don't want to say how much it cost because I still can't believe it wasn't a mistake. Let me just say this: the bill came to more money than tickets to the Panda Parade cost, in total—a lot more. The crib alone cost more than the spending money for my five best friends. I expected my mom to balk or excuse herself to put some of the stuff back or at least pull a coupon out of her gigantic purse. That was what usually happened in this kind of situation. Except not today. As soon as the cashier announced the total, my mom smiled and handed over her credit card.

"Are you sure there hasn't been a mistake?" I asked.

"What do you mean?" My mom frowned down at her list again. "I think we got everything we needed."

"But everything, um . . . ," I started speaking before I realized I didn't know how to complete my thought. "Um, I thought the crib was on back order."

"We pay for it now so they can order it, but it'll come right to the house," said my mom. "Oh, but I'm glad you brought that up."

She turned to the lady at the register and asked, "Is there anyone who can actually assemble the crib?"

The woman said, "For one hundred dollars more you can order white-glove service. That means the delivery person will assemble it for you."

One hundred dollars was the cost of a ticket to the Panda Parade—an entire weekend-long event. And this store was going to charge the same amount of money simply to put together one lousy little crib? Outrageous! I figured my mom would laugh in the cashier's face, but instead she said, "We'll take it," without even blinking.

I'd never seen anything like it.

The cashier handed my mom a form and asked her to fill out our address, and then she swiped my mom's credit card again.

My mom hardly looked at the receipt before she signed it. And a minute later I was pushing the over-flowing shopping cart through the parking lot toward our car.

I started wondering—what if Rachel was right? What if I were rich now and I didn't even know it?

I didn't feel any different. But what does being rich mean, anyway? Is it living in a big house and having a swimming pool? If so, then I guess I was kind of rich. Or at least richer. Did that make me a snob? I didn't think I was better than anyone else. Honestly. I thought I was pretty lucky. There was nothing wrong with feeling lucky, was there?

Not that I felt unlucky before, when it was only me and my mom at home. Things were good then, too, when we lived in North Hollywood. Of course, back then, whenever we'd go to the mall or to Target, my mom clipped coupons. She didn't use one coupon at the Baby Supply Company this afternoon. Maybe my mom didn't care about saving money any-more. The more I thought about it, the more I realized that I hadn't actually seen my mom use a coupon all year.

"Hey, your birthday is coming up, Annabelle. Any thoughts on what you want to do?" my mom asked totally out of the blue.

"I'm not sure," I replied.

"Ted keeps talking about this amazing restaurant in Malibu. And we were thinking maybe we could bring your best friends. It's right on the beach—I'm sure you girls would love it!"

This was unbelievable! "You're not going to suggest we take a limo there, are you?" I asked.

My mom gave me a funny look. "No, that hadn't occurred to me. Do you *want* to take a limo?"

"Of course not!" I said.

"Well, good," she said, as she unlocked the car. "Because that's not really our style."

I looked at the giant cart overflowing with stuff for my new baby brother or sister, wondering what our style was, exactly.

"Um, are we rich?" I asked.

My mom stared at me, confused and a little bit horrified. "Is this about your birthday?" she finally asked. "Because going out to dinner somewhere nice for a special occasion does not mean we're rich. Ted and I just thought since you were turning twelve, you'd want to do something different."

"It's not just about my birthday," I said. "It's a lot of stuff. Because if we are rich, I feel like I should know."

My mom took a deep breath and blinked and stared off into space for a moment before turning back to me. "It's been overwhelming, what with the new big house and all this, um, shopping for the house and for the baby. I know our life is a lot different than it was when we were living on my single salary as a teacher, but everything is relative. We've always had food and clothes and a nice place to live. So I suppose the more direct answer to your question is yes. We have a lot more money than we did before because now we're living on Ted's salary and my salary."

"So we have twice as much money?" I asked.

My mom smiled. "Well, Ted makes more than I do, to be honest with you. So we have more than two of my salaries. But as I said before, everything is relative. Compared to our old apartment, our new house is very large. But compared to the way a lot of people live on this planet, we've always been rich. Do you know how many people don't get enough food to eat? Millions. And do you know how many homeless people there are in the state of California? More than a hundred thousand."

She slammed the trunk and we both got into the car.

As I put my seat belt on I asked, "Did you buy all this stuff when you were pregnant with me?"

"No," she said. "Definitely not. I was on my own with you and I was in graduate school and I was so young. There wasn't much extra money, and I'd never even had a real job before. Your grandmother took care of you so I could finish my degree and get a job at the high school."

"Is it better this time around?" I wondered. "Having more money?"

My mom thought about this for a few moments before answering. "Not better. I'm not going to lie. It's certainly easier not having to worry so much about the future and how I'm going to pay for things. But if I could go back in time and do things differently, I wouldn't. I have no regrets. You are the greatest thing that's ever happened to me. Having another baby is going to make that greatest thing bigger. Two greatest things. Does that answer your question?" she asked.

"Yeah," I said.

"Are things okay with you and your friends?" she asked.

"Of course," I said. "Why?"

"Just making sure. It must be hard for Rachel, not having you across the street anymore. She must feel abandoned."

"I only moved a mile away!" I said. "And it's not like I had a choice in the matter."

"I know, sweetie. She's got to understand that. And if she doesn't now, well, I'm sure she'll come around. But try not to be too hard on her."

"What if she's being hard on me?" I asked.

"Is that where all your questions are coming from?" she asked.

"No comment," I said, crossing my arms over my chest and sinking back into my seat.

chapter eight
the sting of it

Saturday's trouble started at Yumi's, where we all decided to meet at nine a.m. sharp. The morning was gorgeous—the perfect day to have a lemonade stand. At least that was what I thought until we actually set up the lemonade stand.

Claire was fifteen minutes late, but worse than that, even though we'd voted down the muffins less than twenty-four hours before, she'd brought a big Tupperware container filled with them.

"What are those doing here?" asked Yumi.

"Funny story," said Claire. "I was in the mood to bake last night, so I made them. Not for the sale—just to eat. But then my moms asked me to get them out of the house because they're both dieting and they don't want to be tempted, so I had no choice but to bring them with me. Anyway, we don't have to sell them. We can give them away."

Emma shook her head and said, "A, that story isn't funny at all. And B, my whole point yesterday was that muffins are going to make the table too crowded, so giving them away for free does not exactly solve anything."

"Was that your whole point?" asked Claire, tilting her head and squinting at Emma. "I seem to recall you had a bunch of points!"

"Let's not go back there," said Rachel. "Why don't we sell them since they're here already?"

"Did you guys plan this all along?" Emma asked. "Because if you did, well, that's just really sneaky."

"Come on, everyone," I said. "We shouldn't waste time fighting. We've got to get to the playground."

Everyone seemed to agree with me, which was good. But then Claire and Emma reached for the handle of the wagon at the same time and neither wanted to let go.

"I'll get it," Claire snapped.

"That's okay," Emma replied stiffly.

"What, you don't trust me?" asked Claire.

"Fine. Get it," said Emma, letting go and taking a few steps back.

Claire placed her muffin container on top of the fold-up table, which was balanced on top of the beach chairs, which were hovering over the two pitchers of lemonade and the stack of red plastic cups. Then she pulled the wagon along. I dragged the cooler on wheels behind me.

When we were halfway to the park she told us she was ready for a break so Rachel took over. Except Rachel pulled the wagon too fast, and some of the lemonade sloshed out of the pitcher. So Yumi took the wagon instead.

By the time we finally got there, we were all a little sweaty from the heat and a little sticky from the spilled lemonade. Oliver's game didn't start until ten, but I could see his team warming up. He was on the Dodgers, so the uniforms were blue. They were playing the Cardinals, who were in red.

"Let's set up under this tree," said Emma.

"But it's so far from the action," said Yumi, staring at the baseball diamond in the distance.

"I know," said Emma. "But it's right by the parking lot, so every single person who comes to the park will have to pass us at least twice. Plus, we should stick to the shade because it's so hot out today."

"It's going to be eighty-seven degrees, my mom told me," said Emma.

"That's good news for us!" said Claire as she finished setting up the sign.

Yumi and Emma unfolded the two chairs and we all set up the table.

After Claire arranged her mini-muffins, she frowned and said, "Most of the chocolate chips have already melted."

"Oh, that's too bad," said Emma, giving them a quick glance. Except I could tell she didn't mean it.

"That's okay. They still taste delicious," said Claire, popping one in her mouth.

"Don't eat too much of the inventory," Yumi warned.

Claire let out a laugh. "What do you care? You didn't want to sell them in the first place. Remember?"

Rachel reached for one and took a bite. "Delicious!" she said.

"Um, could I try one?" I asked.

"Of course." Claire offered me the container, and I took the smallest-looking muffin.

As soon as I took a bite, the banana-and-chocolate gooey deliciousness practically melted in my mouth. "That's amazing!" I said, polishing off the rest.

"I know. You guys should try one," Claire said to Yumi and Emma.

Yumi went for it, but Emma refused. "No, thanks. I'm not hungry," she said in the primmest voice I've ever heard.

"Come on, Emma. These are some seriously delicious muffins," said Rachel.

Emma sealed her lips tightly and reorganized the table.

Then we got our first customer. Oliver showed up in his baseball uniform—a blue shirt and gray pants with blue kneesocks, and black cleats. He wore his baseball cap low over his forehead and his ears stuck out in the cutest way.

"Good morning," I said brightly. Too brightly? I hoped not.

"Hey, everyone. Cool sign!" he said.

"Thanks," Claire and I said at the same time.

"Claire did most of the work," I admitted, pointing to my friend.

"Well, everyone helped," Claire said shyly.

"I'll take one large lemonade please," he said.

"There's only one size," said Emma, holding up a red cup.

"Okay. Then I guess I'll take it," said Oliver.

"That'll be fifty cents," I said.

He patted the sides of his pants, where his pockets would have been if he actually had pockets on his uniform. "Uh-oh, I don't have any cash on me. Do you take IOUs?"

"Of course," I said at the exact same time that Rachel said, "No way."

I elbowed her.

"Come on, we know Oliver is good for it," I said.

"This is not the way to run a business," said Rachel, pointing to the baseball diamond. "Oliver, surely you could get some money from your mom. Isn't she right over there on the bleachers?"

Oliver raised his eyebrows. He looked not totally offended, but pretty confused. "Um, okay. Be right back."

I turned to Rachel after he jogged off and asked, "Did you really have to do that?"

"Do what?" asked Rachel.

"Treat my boyfriend like a stranger who's out to steal fifty cents' worth of lemonade. You know Oliver will pay us back."

"I know he's not going to steal from our stand intentionally, but he could forget to give us the money. And then where would we be?" asked Rachel. "This is a business. Not a free-lemonade stand. And he's not upset. Look—he's getting the money."

She had a point. Oliver came back less than two minutes later with a dollar. "I'll take two cups now," he said. "My mom wants to try some too."

Rachel glanced at me with raised eyebrows.

"Do not say I told you so," I said as I got Oliver his lemonade. "Seriously. I can't really take the stress right now."

After I handed Oliver his drinks, he took a sip of one and told me it was delicious.

"Thanks!" I said.

"Be sure to tell your friends," Emma called.

"I will," said Oliver. "Good luck, you guys. I've gotta go play ball."

"Knock 'em dead!" I said.

As soon as Oliver left, a bunch of sweaty moms who'd finished their stroller-cizing class came over. Their babies were too young for lemonade, it looked like. But we managed to sell five cups—one to each of them.

Things were going great. The park was plenty busy—there were games being played on all three baseball fields.

We saw some friends from school—Hannah and Tobias came by, separately, and they each bought lemonade. And Sanjay and his little brothers bought three cups. A Girl Scouts troop was having a picnic in the park, so we easily sold ten cups of lemonade to them.

Then Rachel's five-year-old neighbor, Sienna, came by with her mom and they bought two cups. Sienna was smallish and blond, with chunky red-framed glasses.

"This is my friend Annabelle who used to live in your house," Rachel said to them.

Sienna was more interested in the lemonade, but her mom smiled at me and said, "We really love your old place!"

"I'm glad!" I said. "I miss it. I mean, I didn't live there for even a year, but I miss the street and everything."

"It's a lovely street," said Sienna's mom. "And we're so lucky we've got a built-in babysitter."

"What do you mean?" I asked, tilting my head to one side.

"Rachel didn't tell you she's been helping out with Sienna?" asked Sienna's mom.

"This is the best lemonade I've had in ages, isn't it, Mummy?" asked Sienna, holding up the cup.

"It's delicious," said her mom. "Thanks, Rachel. We'll see you tonight, eh?"

"Yup," said Rachel. "I'll be there at five thirty."

Once they left, I asked, "What's that all about?"

"I'm a mother's helper," said Rachel. "I'm taking care of Sienna for two hours tonight."

"That's awesome!" said Yumi. "How much are you getting paid?"

"Five dollars an hour," said Rachel.

"That's great! We'll have ten more dollars for our Panda Parade fund," said Claire.

"Oh, I wasn't going to contribute that money toward the tickets," said Rachel. "I need it for something else."

"But we all pooled our money last week," said Emma. "Remember?"

"I thought that was just to get started," said Rachel. "Anyway, the lemonade stand will earn enough money for the trip. Right, Emma?"

No one really said anything—probably because we didn't know what to say. This was kind of awkward. As I recalled, Rachel hadn't contributed anything last week. This wasn't a big deal, because she hadn't had money at the time. But now she had her allowance plus the money for taking care of Sienna. It only seemed fair that she put it toward the Panda Parade fund. We'd all forked over all our savings, and Yumi was continuing to give us her babysitting earnings. Why wasn't Rachel doing the same?

I didn't ask, though, because I didn't want to get into another fight with Rachel about money. Probably she'd say something like I didn't really need my savings because my mom bought me whatever it was that I wanted. It wasn't true, but I didn't want to open myself up to another attack.

A bunch more people came over to buy lemonade, and it seemed as if our stand was a big success, but thinking about Rachel put me in a rotten mood, so I couldn't enjoy it. Even though we didn't actually have this fight in real life, our pretend fight in my head was pretty bad, and I couldn't help but be annoyed with her all over again.

An hour later, when Oliver's game ended, both teams cheered and then gave each other high fives.

The other baseball games seemed to be breaking up too.

Claire said, "Everyone, get ready!"

We sat up straighter, ready for the onslaught. Thirty boys in baseball uniforms were walking straight toward us. They all looked thirsty.

"It's rush hour!" I exclaimed.

"This is what we've been waiting for!" said Rachel.

"I wish we had more muffins," said Claire.

"I have to agree," said Emma. "They were good."

"When did you have one?" asked Claire.

"I snuck it when no one was looking. Sorry!" Emma flashed Claire a guilty smile.

"Told you they were great," said Claire, throwing her arm around Emma's shoulders and giving her a squeeze.

Oliver was leading the pack, bringing the entire team over and not just that—parents, too.

"Hey, do you want some more lemonade?" I asked, all ready to pour him a cup.

"No, thanks." Oliver held up a big can of Limonata and said, "We all got these after the game."

"Oh," I said, my smile fading as I noticed the boys. Some were drinking Limonata. Some were drinking Capri Sun. Some had bottles of water or Gatorade. But all of them had something to drink.

"Do you mind going away?" Rachel asked rudely, shooing Oliver.

"Rachel, what is going on with you?" I asked.

"What's going on with *you*?" she replied. "How come you're letting your boyfriend mess with our stand?"

"How is he messing with the stand? He was our first customer. Do I need to remind you that he bought two lemonades?"

Oliver looked back and forth between us, totally confused.

Rachel angrily pointed at him. "You're standing in front of our sign, drinking a huge sip of lemonade from somewhere else."

"Limonata is more like a soda," said Oliver. "Plus, Annabelle just reminded you that I already bought yours."

"There's no limit. You could totally buy more, which would be much healthier than that lemon-flavored soda," said Rachel. "Ours is sweetened with agave nectar."

I couldn't believe how she was acting. My other friends had backed away a bit. My guess was that they were surprised by her strong reaction.

"Rachel," I said gently.

"What?" she snapped. "The whole point of the lemonade stand is to earn money, right? I know you don't need it, but there are other people with a lot at stake."

"What's that supposed to mean?" I asked.

"You know Ted is rich and he would buy your concert ticket if you asked him to."

"That's not true," I said. "We're all in this together."

"Some of us are more in it than others," she said.

"You're right," I said. "And some of us are still contributing all our money!"

"You guys, stop fighting!" said Emma.

"We're not fighting!" Rachel and I shouted at the same time.

We hung out at the park for another hour and sold a few more cups of lemonade. But by two o'clock, the park was empty.

"I think it's too hot for lemonade," said Emma. "If that's possible. Maybe we should just pack our things up and go home."

"I agree," said Claire. "But let's count our profits first, so we at least know all our hard work was worth it."

This seemed like a good idea, so Emma opened up our cash box and began counting.

There seemed to be a lot of dimes and nickels in the box, and not so many dollars. This was not a good sign, but I kept my hopes up. Claire crossed her fingers as we all stared at the money.

Moments later Emma looked up, distressed. "We only made eleven dollars. That means we sold twenty-two cups of lemonade."

"After four hours of work? We made less than two dollars an hour and that's among the five of us."

"So each of us made about thirty-six cents an hour," said Claire. "We could make more money than that looking for change in our living room couch cushions."

"We can try again next weekend," I said. "I've still got plenty of lemons on my tree."

We all looked to Emma, who was doing some calculations in her notebook. "Sorry, guys. Even if we double our sales next weekend we still won't make enough money in time. We need a new plan."

Everyone snapped to attention and looked at Yumi, who was cradling her right hand, real tears streaming down her face.

I tried reassuring her. "It's not so bad," I said. "We still have plenty of time to raise the money."

"It's not that!" she yelled. "I got stung by a bee!"

chapter nine

Yumi is not allergic to bees, which is pretty much the best thing that happened today. And when your best friend *not* being hospitalized for a life-threatening allergy is the highlight of your day, you know it was pretty rotten.

We hurried back to her house, and her mom pulled out the stinger and gave us some Neosporin and a Band-Aid. Then we headed back outside and sat down on Yumi's front lawn in the shade. None of us spoke for a while—we were all too hot and sticky and exhausted, not to mention seriously depressed.

"So what's the new plan?" asked Rachel.

"Yeah, we need to figure something out," said Claire.

Yumi examined her Band-Aid, while Rachel picked a blade of grass, folded it, put it to her lips, and tried to whistle.

Then, before any of us had the chance to speak, a red station wagon drove by. It was old and dirty and spewing smoke out of its tailpipe.

"That car is so gross," Claire whispered.

"Shh," said Rachel. "They'll hear you."

"They can't hear with the windows up," Claire said.

"You never know," I said. "Plus, it's rude to say that. Maybe they can't afford a better car."

"The car is fine. My point is, it's filthy, and anyone who has a car can afford to keep it clean," said Claire.

Suddenly my ears perked up and my brain began to whir as a new plan unfolded—a plan with an extra dose of awesome-sauce.

Most cars needed a serious washing at some point. And every single kid I knew had a parent with a car. Some people I knew even had extra cars. And all those cars had to get clean, which meant one thing. . . .

I stood up and raised my fists above my head in a cheer for victory. "Hey, I know. We can have our own car wash!"

And that's how we ended up in the parking lot of Home Depot the following Sunday. Yumi's neighbor was the manager of the store, and he gave us permission to set up in front of it.

Home Depot was the best place to be because everyone went there on the weekend. At least that was what Ted told me.

And it did seem perfect—I had a really good feeling about things. We'd spent Saturday afternoon getting ready and everything had been a snap. All we needed were five giant buckets, a bunch of sponges, rags, and carwash soap, and a hose. Oh, and a uniform—that was Emma's idea. She thought we'd look more professional if our clothes matched. And luckily we all had jean shorts and green T-shirts. Claire managed to recycle our lemonade stand sign. Now the gigantic tie-dye sheet read, CAR WASH FOR PANDAS. TEN BUCKS! With the five of us lined up in front, we looked like old pros.

"This is going to be awesome!" I said a few minutes before the Home Depot officially opened.

"I know—the profit ratio is much higher," said Emma. "We can charge ten dollars per wash. That means we only have to wash seventy-five cars to reach our goal."

"Seventy-five cars is a lot," said Claire. "Me and Olivia washed our moms' two cars a few weeks ago, and it took us all morning."

"Maybe you should sell some muffins, too," said Emma. "People can eat them while they wait!"

Claire thought about this for a moment. "I suppose it could work," she said.

"I'm kidding!" said Emma.

"Oh," said Claire. "Sorry!" She glanced at her watch. "What time does the store open?"

"In five minutes," said Yumi, blinking as she looked out at the sea of asphalt. The parking lot was empty except for us.

Rachel had brought along an old boom box so at least we had music. The radio was tuned to our favorite station, and after a bunch of commercials, we finally got to hear a familiar song: "When You Left" by Kylie Granger. It was sort of half country and half rock and all great.

Also? It was the kind of song that was so catchy, I couldn't help dancing—even on a Sunday morning in the middle of a parking lot.

Luckily, my friends seemed to feel the same way. None of us could keep still, so we basically became a five-person, parking-lot dance party.

After the song, the DJ came on and said, "Kylie Granger is kicking off her summer tour and she'll be appearing at the Panda Parade in Indio in six short weeks. Tickets are on sale now!"

"Kylie Granger is going to be in Indio too?" asked Claire. "It keeps getting better and better. I so wish we could buy tickets now."

Emma frowned at the radio. "Me too. And I just had a terrible thought. What if they sell out before we raise the money?"

"Ugh, the pressure," Rachel said, holding her head in her hands.

"I know. He had to remind us that we only have six weeks left," I agreed.

"I'm sure the cars will arrive any minute now," said Claire. "And we'll be on our way!"

All five of us stared in anxious anticipation at the

entrance to the parking lot. It'd been almost an hour since we'd gotten set up. Sure, we were having fun, but it would've been nice if we could have fun while washing cars and making some ticket money.

After a few moments of nothing, Emma asked, "Have you guys ever heard that old saying, 'A watched pot never boils'?"

"Are you implying that if we keep staring at the parking lot entrance, no one's gonna come?" asked Yumi.

Emma shrugged. "Sort of."

"You're right," Yumi said with a nod as she read-justed her baseball cap. "We've gotta find something else to do. I should've brought a ball so we could play catch or something."

"Maybe we don't need a ball," I said, staring at the buckets lined up on the sidewalk. Each was filled to the brim with soapy water and a giant sponge. I took out one of the sponges, wrung out as much water as I could, and took a bunch of steps back. Then I tossed the sponge into the bucket, where it landed with a splash.

"Yes!" I said, raising both hands above my head. "It's car wash basketball!"

"Nice one," said Claire. "Let me try." She took her own sponge out of the bucket and stepped backward about six paces.

"I think it's too easy from there," I said. "Why not move back a few more steps?"

"Okay." Claire took five giant steps backward, aimed, and shot. Her sponge hit the side of the bucket but bounced off.

"Close," I said.

"Let me try next," said Rachel, grabbing the sponge off the ground and moving back to where we stood.

She shot and made it in the bucket, and we all cheered. Then Emma said, "Guys, look. It's a car!"

An old truck pulled into the parking lot, and a man and a woman got out. They were both dressed up. He wore a suit and she was in a lavender dress.

"Would you like us to wash your car while you shop?" asked Claire.

"It's only ten dollars," I added.

"We're raising money for pandas," said Yumi, coughing. "Well, indirectly. We're trying to buy concert tickets for a show benefiting panda bears."

"They're endangered," Rachel said.

The man smiled at us. "Oh, I wish I'd come here first, but I just got the car washed earlier this morning." He wasn't making things up: his truck gleamed in the sun. There wasn't a spot on it.

"Good luck to you all," said the woman he was with.

"Thanks," I said with a wave.

They strolled on into the store, hand in hand.

"What a cute couple," said Yumi. "I can see me

and Nathan shopping for hardware together when we are grown up and living in the same time zone."

"I thought you guys broke up again," said Rachel.

"Yeah, that was yesterday," said Yumi. "But as of this morning we're back together again. He texted me at six a.m. to ask me out."

"That's so early!" I said.

"It was eight o'clock in Michigan," said Yumi.

Right then another car came into the lot—this one was a shiny silver Mercedes SUV. Shiny, as in clean and sparkly, so we didn't even bother asking if the owner wanted it washed. Clearly, he didn't need it.

Six cars later, though, a dirty old Ford pickup pulled in. I think it was navy blue, but it was hard to tell underneath all the grime.

"Finally!" said Claire. She pulled her hair up into a bun on top of her head and readjusted her headband.

Then the five us ran toward the car, making it there before anyone even managed to climb out.

"Can we wash your car?" asked Claire.

The driver had long blond braids and bright blue eyes. She wore skinny jeans and a white tank top. "Oh, a car wash. Awesome, I totally need that, but I don't have enough cash at the moment," she said. "Do you take credit cards?"

We sighed collectively. "Not exactly," said Emma. "But do you have any cash? Because we can negotiate."

The lady dug in her purse and pulled out two quarters and a penny. "This is all I've got."

We stared at the fifty-one cents. A penny more than we'd sold a cup of lemonade for.

"I don't think we can wash your car for that," said Emma. "I wish we could take credit cards. I didn't even think about that."

"So sorry!" she called as she waltzed off with her hands in her pockets.

We stared at her dirty car and then at the parking lot, which was not as busy as we'd expected it to be.

"I don't get it," I said. "This plan seemed perfect, foolproof. Amazing."

"Wait," said Emma. "I think we're in business."

She pointed to the parking lot entrance as five—count 'em, five—cars pulled in at once. And none of them was exactly spotless.

We decided to spread out, so we could each hit up one of the drivers.

I walked over to a lady in a blue sundress and heels getting out of a black minivan. "We're washing cars for ten dollars," I said. "Are you interested?"

"I wish I could," she said, as she tucked her purse under her arm. "But my church is doing a car wash fundraiser today, and I need to get it done there."

"Your church is washing cars?" I asked.

"Yes," she said. "All Saints does it every Sunday for the months of May and June. It's a tradition, not to mention one of our biggest fundraisers."

"Um, where is All Saints?" I asked.

"Right down the block," she said, pointing to the left. "You know the large brick building with the white cross on top? It's the biggest church in town."

"Oh," I said. "Well, thanks anyway. And good luck to you."

"You too!" she said. She raised her hand to shade her eyes from the sun as she squinted at our sign. "Oh, you're raising money for pandas? I love pandas!"

"Me too," I said.

She dug into her purse and came up with a dollar. "Please add this to your fund. And I'm sorry I can't have you wash my car, but my nephews are waiting for me at All Saints."

"It's no problem," I said. "Um, thank you for your donation."

I jogged back to my friends, hoping they'd have better luck than I did.

"So?" I asked Yumi, who was already there.

"No dice," she told me, shaking her head. "My dude said he didn't have time, and I promised him we'd be fast, but he said maybe another time. So I told him we'd probably be back next weekend although I don't know." She glanced at her watch. "It's already ten forty-five and we haven't made a dime."

I pulled the crumpled dollar out of my shorts pocket and showed it to Yumi. "We've made ten dimes!"

Yumi's eyes got way wide as she looked back and forth between me and the minivan. "We're washing that lady's car for a dollar?" she asked.

"No, she just gave me a donation. She's going to All Saints to have her car washed."

Yumi's shoulders slumped in disappointment, and I knew exactly how she felt.

A few moments later Emma came over. "Don't tell me," she said, her voice flat with disappointment. "The people in your cars already have plans to get their cars washed by the high school cheerleaders at the grocery store."

"No, at All Saints," I said. "Wait, the cheerleaders are having a car wash as well?"

"Yup," said Emma, wiping some sweat off her brow with the back of her hand. "It would've been great to know about that yesterday, before we sprung for supplies."

"What do we do?" I asked once the rest of us regrouped.

"We need to stay here and stick it out," said Rachel. "It hasn't even been an hour."

"Hey, look," I said. "It's my mom."

My mom pulled up next to us and climbed out of her car. "You girls look fantastic!" she said.

"That's actually bad news, Mrs. Stevens," said Emma. "We're so clean because we haven't washed any cars yet."

"Well, please wash mine—I'm in desperate need of a power drill and a car wash," she said. "And I'm pretty excited I get to take care of both chores in one place." Once she climbed out of her car, she fished around in her purse until she found a twenty.

"Here you go," she said.

"Oh, we don't have change yet," I said. "Sorry!"

"Want us to wash it twice?" Claire joked.

My mom laughed. "No, why don't you girls keep the change? I know the money is going toward a good cause."

"Okay!" Emma said, putting my mom's twenty in the cash box.

A little while later, Rachel's and Yumi's moms showed up.

So in hour three we made forty-one dollars, although we hadn't actually washed a car that belonged to someone who hadn't given birth to one of us.

Finally an actual stranger came up to us. "You're washing cars?" he asked.

"Yup. For ten dollars," said Emma.

"Okay," said the man. He pointed out his truck, which was parked at the far end of the lot. It was caked in dirt and mud, and it was definitely the dirtiest car I'd ever seen in my whole entire life.

"Good luck!" he said, handing us exact change.

We carried our supplies over to his truck and got

to work scrubbing and rinsing and scrubbing some more. Somehow, instead of merely cleaning the car, we came out looking as if we'd magically transferred all the filth from his car onto our bodies. And it turned out that his car had plenty of filth for the five of us! The car looked great and the dude was so thrilled, he gave us a two-dollar tip.

We hung out at the Home Depot parking lot for another hour, and we managed to wash two more cars. By the end of the day all our ponytails had drooped. We were sunburned and exhausted and wet and tired.

"What's that smell?" asked Claire.

"Oh, that's me," said Emma. "My deodorant isn't built for this kind of work!"

"To be fair, I think it's all of us," said Yumi.

"How much do you think we made?" I wondered.

"Three hundred," said Claire. "Maybe four."

"I think two hundred and fifty is more accurate," said Yumi.

"Well, that's still pretty good," said Rachel.

"Maybe we'll be able to buy the tickets tonight," I said. Then I reconsidered. "Or maybe after next weekend. Then we can retire."

"That would be awesome," Emma said, wiping her forehead with the back of her hand. "Let's count so we know for sure."

We all headed over to the corner of the parking lot

where we had our sign and extra supplies. Emma reached for our cash box and opened it up.

Then she began smoothing out the bills and counting. This took a while, since most of them were crumpled or folded, and some were even damp. But we were patient—all five of us kept our eyes on the money.

"And seventy-three," Emma finished. She dug around the box and lifted up the top tray in search of stray bills, but there were none.

We looked at the pile of cash. So many bills added up to so little money.

"It's not that bad," said Claire. "Right?"

"It's fine," Emma said. "Definitely a huge improvement over last weekend, but it's not going to get us to the Panda Parade anytime soon."

"Should we try again next weekend?" I asked.

"I don't know if it's worth it," said Emma. "The All Saints car wash is happening for the next five weekends, and it's the biggest church in town. If we make seventy-three dollars every weekend for the next five weekends, that only comes to three hundred and sixty-five dollars—less than half of what we need."

"So what are you saying?" asked Claire.

Emma sighed as she emptied a bucket of dirty water into the gutter. "I'm saying, doing the same thing every weekend is too risky. We need to think of something else."

Just then a Taylor Swift song came on the radio, but instead of dancing to it, this time Rachel turned the music off. "I can't believe we failed again," she said.

"Well, it could be worse," said Yumi. "At least no one got injured today."

chapter ten
who's afraid of the dark?

My mom teaches high-school English. She has ever since I can remember. But on Monday night, over dinner, she told me she was going to take next year off. This news was so shocking to me, I almost dropped my fork.

"The entire year?" I asked. "What are you going to do?"

"Well, the baby will keep me busy," she said.

"Oh, right," I said, staring at her stomach. It seemed to be getting bigger and bigger by the day—if that were possible.

It was weird thinking about a human being growing inside her. And it was almost weirder for me to think about my mom not working and being at home all the time. When I was first born, she was in school and she finished nights, and my grandparents baby-sat for me. Then I went into day care so she could teach. Even in the summer, she usually taught summer school. As long as I'd been alive, she'd never not worked.

"Are you sure you're *allowed* to take a year off?" I asked. "What if they don't let you come back?"

My mom laughed. "Yes, I'm allowed, and I will go back. I worked it all out. I've been teaching for ten years straight—the school is willing to give me this time."

"Oh," I said. And I guess I had a pensive expression on my face because suddenly my mom ruffled my hair.

"Don't worry so much, Annabelle. The baby will be sleeping a lot, so I'll have plenty of time for you. We can hang out all the time. It'll be so much fun!"

I laughed at first, figuring my mom was kidding. Except by the look on her face, I realized she wasn't.

My mom really wanted to hang out with me all the time? Yikes! This was not exactly ideal. Don't get me wrong—I love my mom. A lot. She's my mom. Plus, she's fun and cool and easygoing as far as moms are concerned. But that didn't mean I wanted to spend the entire summer with her. I had a life—tons of friends and a boyfriend, too. I tried to think of a way to remind her of this, without being rude. But I couldn't. Anyway, my phone was vibrating in my back pocket. I pulled it out and read a text from Oliver: *What's up?*

"No phones at the dinner table, sweetheart," Ted gently reminded me.

"Sorry," I said, looking up. "Um, may I please be excused?"

"Are you finished eating or just wanting to call your boyfriend?" my mom asked.

"How'd you know it was Oliver calling?" I wondered. "And for that matter, how did you know that Oliver was my boyfriend?"

"I could tell by the way you swooned," she said.

"I did not swoon," I said.

Ted laughed.

"I didn't," I insisted. "Whatever swooning means. And by the way—I'm done eating *and* I want to call Oliver back. The two aren't mutually exclusive."

"Well, then," said Ted. "I guess you are free to go."

I cleared my plate and ran upstairs and called Oliver.

"Hey," he said.

"Hey," I replied.

"Want to shoot some hoops?" he asked.

"Sure, but my hoop isn't up yet," I told him.

"Too bad," said Oliver. "Want to do something else?"

"Yeah," I said. "Like what?"

"I don't know. How about if I come over and we can figure it out?"

I smiled. "Okay."

"Cool—I'll meet you in front of your house in five."

After we hung up I went to the bathroom and checked myself in the mirror. My hair was kind of tangled, probably from when my mom rumpled it— I'd have to get her to stop doing that. I ran my brush through it a bunch of times. But then it got all flyaway and static-y, so I ended up pulling it into a ponytail, which I turned into a loose bun on the top of my head. I changed out of my new jeans and into some older jeans because I didn't want to seem too dressed up. And then I ran downstairs to wait outside on my front lawn for Oliver.

My lawn slopes down to the sidewalk, and I sat at the top of it, cross-legged, my elbows on my knees and my chin resting on my knuckles. I tried to look casual, as if my stomach weren't fluttering like crazy. It was fun having Oliver right down the street. We'd probably be hanging out like this a lot. Rachel and I used to meet outside after dinner on lots of nights too, back when I lived across the street from her.

I wondered what Rachel was doing now. Even though I'd been annoyed with her lately, I still missed her. Also, I'd been thinking about the situation a lot, and I guess I could understand her being upset that I moved away, but it didn't excuse her behavior. As I'd told her before, I didn't ask my parents to move away. I had no choice in the matter.

I was tired of her snide little comments. They always left me with this weird hollowed-out feeling inside. Not to mention a gazillion questions.

How could moving from one end of town to the other—simply a mile away—turn me into a snob? It seemed completely impossible. So where did her idea even come from? Or was I taking Rachel's comments too seriously? Maybe she had been kidding around this whole time. Everyone makes a bad joke on occasion. Maybe she was having a week's worth of bad jokes.

Of course, someone once said to me that every single joke contained a kernel of truth. If that were the case, where was the truth in what Rachel was saying? I was the furthest thing from a snob in the whole entire universe. And I wasn't rich. It was true: we'd moved to a bigger house—and okay, the new neighborhood was nicer too. Or at least, it was filled with bigger houses. I wasn't sure if that made it nicer or not. Nicer seemed like a matter of opinion. My old house had been perfectly nice; same with the tiny apartment I had lived in with my mom before that, before Ted came into our lives.

But none of those facts had anything to do with me. Where I lived didn't make me who I was. And by the way, if you hadn't figured it out already—I was a very nice, not-at-all-snobby kid. I knew all this to be true, but I wasn't about to say it out loud in front of all my friends. Why did I need to defend myself? They all knew the truth about me, and that's why we were friends in the first place.

When Oliver showed up, he said, "Hey, sorry to keep you waiting. My mom made me take out the trash first and some of her coffee grinds got all over my sweatshirt and I had to change."

"That's okay," I said.

He got down on the lawn next to me, leaning back on his elbows with his legs kicked out in front of him. "Hey, are you okay?"

"Fine," I said. "Why?"

"You seemed upset when I first saw you."

"No, I was just thinking."

"About what?"

"About Rachel. And how I used to live across the street from her. And how she's kind of acting all mad now that I don't, even though it's not my fault."

It felt good, being so honest with Oliver. I couldn't really talk to any of my friends about the problem because my friends were Rachel's friends too.

"It's dumb for her to be mad at you for things you can't control," said Oliver. "It's not like you asked your parents to move away from her and closer to me. Although I'm glad you did."

"I'm glad I did too," I said. "But it's not only the fact that I moved. She's acting like just because I live in Canyon Ranch now, I'm a snob, and she's treating me differently. And I haven't changed, have I?"

"Actually, I've been meaning to talk to you about that," said Oliver. He had the most serious expression on his face, like he was about to give me horrible news. "You have changed, and I feel as if I don't know you anymore."

"What?" I cried.

Just then he smiled, and his slow smile turned

into a laugh. He clapped his hands once. "I totally got you, Annabelle!"

I punched Oliver's arm.

"Ouch!" he said, rubbing it.

"That didn't hurt," I said. "And if it did—good. You totally deserved it."

He laughed again. "Come on, I was only having fun."

"But this is serious. Rachel's, like, my very best friend."

"Then you need to talk to her," he said.

"But what do I say? 'I don't like your jokes'? They hurt my feelings. It's hard to know when she'll be nice or mean, so I'm always caught off guard."

"Do you want me to talk to her?" he asked. "Because I totally will."

Getting Oliver involved seemed weird and unnecessary, but I still felt flattered that he offered, like he wanted to protect me or something. It was sweet. Even though I knew I had to handle this myself, I was still curious.

"What would you say?" I asked.

"Back off my girlfriend," said Oliver in a fake-tough guy voice as he shook his fists. "Or else there'll be trouble."

I laughed.

"What? I don't sound super-intimidating?" he asked. "Should I flex my muscles instead?"

"What muscles?" I asked.

This time Oliver socked me in the arm.

"Ouch!" I said. "Okay, no more punching. Truce?"

"Truce," he repeated.

We shook hands and I smiled at him. "You're too sweet to sound intimidating, and I mean that as a compliment."

Oliver shrugged. "Whatever. I hate to see you upset. It's not fair. I think you need to talk to her. Honesty is the best policy. I know that's a cliché, but it's true."

"I wish it were that simple," I said with a sigh. "But don't worry. I'll be fine."

"Okay," he said. "Hey, want to see this new trick I learned on my skateboard?"

"Sure."

He got up and ran back to his house and came back with his skateboard, which was black with a purple skeleton face on the top and neon green wheels. He was also sporting a matching helmet.

"Don't laugh about the helmet," he said. "My mom makes me wear it."

"That's okay," I said. "It's probably a good idea."

Oliver got a serious look on his face as he buckled the chin strap on his helmet. Then he headed to the top of my driveway. "Ready?" he asked.

"Yup," I replied.

Suddenly he raced straight down, and when there were only a few feet between him and the street, he veered left, bent down to catch the edge of his board, and hopped off the curb.

It was amazing and totally impressive for about two seconds. Then he lost control and wobbled, yelling with his arms flailing, before face-planting on the street.

I scrambled to my feet and ran over. "Are you okay?" I asked.

He stood up quickly and bent down to check out his knee, which was bleeding. "Ow!" he said. His chin was scraped up too, but not as badly.

"That was an awesome attempt," I said.

"I did it perfectly this morning—five times in a row."

"Sorry I missed it," I said.

"Your driveway must be different from mine," Oliver said, standing up straighter. "Let me try again."

"But you're bleeding."

"It's not so bad," he said, wiping his knee with the back of his hand and then wiping his hand on his shorts. He picked up his board and hurried to the top of the driveway. And I sat back down again, watching him repeat the entire trick. This time he pulled it off flawlessly, landing on the board and coasting down the street.

"Yay!" I said, clapping.

Oliver turned around and skated back to me with the biggest grin on his face. "Want to see it again?" he asked.

I glanced at his bloody knee. "Um, why don't you quit while you're ahead?"

"I'm actually tied—one fall and one jump," he said.

"And you still have one unbruised knee," I pointed out.

Oliver looked down at his knees. "Oh, this is nothing," he said. "You should've seen me last summer when I first got this thing."

Except before Oliver could jump again, Ted called to me from the front door. "Annabelle, your mom wants you inside now."

I stood up and brushed the grass off my shorts. "How come?" I asked.

"Something about it being a school night," he said. "And the sun going down."

"It's okay," said Oliver, standing up and tucking his skateboard under one arm. "I should get home too."

"See you tomorrow," I said.

"Want to walk to school together?"

"Sure," I said, smiling. As soon as I found out I was moving onto Oliver's street, I was hoping we'd get to walk to school together. But so far I'd been too shy to bring it up myself.

"I'll come by at seven thirty-five," he said.

"And I'll be ready. See you then."

We waved good-bye, and I walked over to where Ted was still standing by the front door. "I can't stay out after dark, even if I'm on my own front lawn?" I asked.

"Apparently not," said Ted with a shrug. "I don't make the rules around here—I just follow them. You know that."

"Huh," I said. "I'll have to talk to my mom about that. It's not like I'm going to turn into a pumpkin when the sun goes down."

"Maybe your mom's afraid of vampires."

"Oh, Ted," I said. "Vampires are so five years ago."

"Werewolves, then," said Ted.

"Vampires and werewolves went out of fashion at the same time."

"Okay, how about zombies?" asked Ted.

I yawned, bored with the conversation. "That's last year."

"Then what's the new evil monster out to get you?" he asked.

"I don't even know yet," I said, although I actually did: the new evil monster out to get me was my very best friend.

Or should I now refer to Rachel as my former best friend?

chapter eleven
mystery text

Two days later I was curled up in bed with Pepper at my feet, finishing up my lab report and about to crack open my history book when Ted knocked on my door.

"Come in," I said.

"Hey, how's it going?" he asked. "Guess what? I have a surprise for you."

"Is the trampoline up?" I asked, looking out my window. Scanning the backyard, I saw only the green grass, the sparkling blue pool, and the raised beds my mom had bought for her future vegetable garden. I wondered if maybe the new trampoline was in the front yard and Ted hadn't set it up yet.

"Nope, the trampoline is on back order, but it'll be here in ten days. I have something else."

He reached into his back pocket and pulled out his iPhone. "This is for you."

"Really?" I asked. "This is awesome! But wait. Don't you need it?"

"I upgraded to the new one," said Ted. "And I was

all ready to trade this one in, but then I realized you could use it."

I'd seen iPhones before. My mom and Ted had them and so did my uncle Steve.

Come to think of it, Oliver had one, as did a few other kids at my school, but it definitely wasn't the norm. Like, just the fact that I could name all the kids who had iPhones said something about owning one. Namely, the phones are super-fancy. They were a cool shape—thin and rectangular—and the screen was in color. I could text and listen to music and take and store pictures. Some of that stuff my old phone did, but I knew the iPhone did it all better. Plus, I could now e-mail from my phone. Not that I e-mail very often or anything. The only people who e-mail me are my grandma and my uncle. But still, it was good to have the capability. I'd never had it before.

"Want me to show you how to use it?" asked Ted.

"Oh, I know how," I said. "My friend has this phone."

I could've said, "My boyfriend has this phone," but it felt strange talking about my boyfriend in front of Ted or any grown-up for that matter. Even though it was no secret that I had a boyfriend, I was still getting used to the fact, and talking about him casually felt too weird. Good weird, usually, but still weird, and best to be avoided when grown-ups were around.

"Good," said Ted. "Let me transfer your data for you. Also, since you can now listen to music from this, I'll give you my old speakers."

"You don't need them?" I asked.

"I can't use them with the new version of the phone, so I had to upgrade those, too."

"Oh," I said. It was sweet and super-generous and thoughtful of Ted to give me his old stuff. Which wasn't even that old. It was pretty new and nicer than what my friends had. And there was the problem right there.

I thought about what this would mean, what would happen if I showed up to school tomorrow with a brand-new phone. It would be fun and exciting probably, showing it to everyone. But was it also too showy? Would Rachel give me a hard time? Only this morning she had asked me if my shirt was new. It wasn't at all—I'd worn it before in front of her. But she seemed to be looking for things to fight about. She'd convinced herself I'd changed since my move, so everything I did, no matter what it was, somehow became evidence to prove I was a different person now.

Did other kids feel this way too? Did I seem rich, and did that therefore make me a snob? Did simply living in Canyon Ranch change things? I didn't want to be seen as a shallow snob or as materialistic. If I was getting my stepdad's old, used phone, why was I even worried about this? It wasn't like I had even asked for it.

I guess I'd been pretty quiet for a while because

all of a sudden Ted asked, "Everything okay, Anna-banana?"

"Fine," I said. "Thanks for the phone. It's awe-some!"

"And guess what? I downloaded the new Lobster Lips album for you. I know you're excited about see-ing them at the Panda Parade."

"Ha! If we get to go," I said. "You heard about the car wash disaster?"

"I wouldn't call it a disaster," said Ted. "But yes, I heard it was a bit of a disappointment."

"We tried really hard to raise the money," I said. "Some of my friends are hoping all our parents will see that and spring for the tickets. You know, kind of like giving us an A for effort?"

"Well, you definitely get an A for effort," said Ted. "But we're not backing down, and I know you girls will figure something out. The concert is still six weeks away."

As soon as Ted plugged in the iPhone and put on the new song, I got a text on my old phone. It was from Claire.

I am brilliant! she wrote.

And so modest, I replied.

Drop everything you are doing, find some old socks, and come over IMMEDIATELY!!!

Huh? I asked.

Three words: sock puppet monkeys!!!

I texted back two rows of question marks.

Just come, Claire wrote back. *I'll explain in person.*

"Mind if you transfer the phone data later? I need to go to Claire's for a little while. It's kind of an emergency."

Ted laughed as he looked at his watch. "What kind of emergency?"

I glanced back down at my phone. "I'm not really sure, but it's important."

"Okay, but make sure you're home before dark. You know—so the vampires don't get you."

I smiled at Ted, asking, "Haven't we been over this already?"

chapter twelve
leave them in stitches!

I threw a few pairs of old socks into my backpack, hopped on my trusty red ten-speed, and biked over to Claire's house. By the time I got there, she and Yumi were waiting on the front lawn.

"So what's the big plan?" I asked as I skidded to a stop, climbed off my bike, and carefully placed it on its side, since my kickstand was busted.

Claire's cheeks were flushed and her blue eyes sparkled with excitement. "We've got to wait until everyone else gets here," she said.

"I can hardly stand the suspense," said Yumi.

"Did you bring your old mismatched socks?" asked Claire.

"Of course," I said, pulling them out of my bag to show her. "I wasn't sure of how many to bring so I grabbed all the ones I could find."

"See," Claire said to Yumi. "My text was perfectly clear."

"I thought she was kidding," Yumi explained to me.

"Well, I wasn't sure," I admitted. "But I figured it's better to be safe than sockless."

"Hey, I learned my lesson. That's totally going to be my new motto in life," Yumi said.

"Don't worry—I've got plenty to spare," Claire assured her.

Yumi adjusted her baseball cap and asked, "How many do we need?"

"A bunch," Claire said mysteriously.

"Are we making some kind of giant rope out of old socks?" asked Yumi, tilting her head to the side and squinting at Claire as if trying to figure out a puzzle.

Claire laughed. "How would that get us to the Panda Parade?"

Yumi shrugged. "Honestly, I have no idea."

This was getting more intriguing by the second. Luckily, Rachel and Emma arrived a minute later so Claire could finally reveal her big plan.

Wearing the most sparkling smile I've ever seen, she stood up, placed her hands on her hips and announced, "We are going to make and sell sock puppet monkeys."

Claire's declaration was met with silence. I could tell she was expecting some kind of humungous reaction, but none of us knew what to say. All we could do was stare at her and then at one another, at least at first.

Finally Rachel coughed and asked, "Um, what's a sock puppet monkey?"

"You know," said Claire. "It's a puppet made out of a sock."

Claire seemed way enthusiastic, but the rest of us were still pretty confused.

"So you think we're going to pay for the Panda Parade trip by selling old socks?" asked Rachel.

"I told you they're not just socks," Claire explained, somewhat frustrated. "They're totally tricked-out socks. Or they will be. All we've got to do is add eyes and a nose and hair and maybe some cute clothes. We'll decorate them and make them super-cute. They don't all have to be monkeys, either. We can make sock puppet puppies and bunnies and elephants—even sock-puppet people. I've got a ton of old buttons we can use for eyes, and yarn for hair. Also, they don't have to be puppets. We can just stuff them with a lot of cotton and sell them as custom-made, one-of-a-kind dolls. That might be better, actually. We can experiment—make them whatever we want them to be. It'll be fun!"

"But who are we going to sell them to?" I had to ask.

"Everyone!" said Claire, throwing out her hands.

"Okay," Emma said, looking at Claire nervously. It was the kind of look you might give to an insane person, which wasn't entirely inappropriate at the moment. "But where are we going to sell them?"

"At school," Claire said, like it was obvious.

"You think our classmates will want them?" asked Rachel.

"If we make them cute enough," Claire said with a shrug. "Of course. Let's get started."

We all looked at one another again. Each of us seemed to be mulling over the idea. I couldn't tell what anyone else was thinking, and to be honest—I wasn't exactly sure how I felt about the idea.

"It's too quiet," said Claire. "Someone say something!"

I forced a smile and shrugged, trying to come up with something to say. "It's definitely, um, original. And it's not the worst idea. . . ."

Emma nodded slowly. "Good point, Annabelle. Plus, it's the only idea on the table at the moment."

"I guess that makes it a winner," said Yumi. "So let's go for it!"

Claire jumped up and down and clapped. "This is going to be awesome, guys, and I'm not just saying that because it's my idea. I really think we're on to something. Come with me."

We followed Claire into her dining room, where she'd set up all her art supplies. Her laptop was there too. "Okay, you guys. I found this great video on You-Tube on how to make sock puppet monkeys."

"You really did your homework," said Emma.

"Of course I did—this is important," said Claire.

Emma nodded with approval. "I think we should make some sock puppet pandas. You know, since we're going to sell them so we can go to the Panda Parade. It'll be good luck."

"Great idea!" said Claire. "You should totally go for it, and I've got a black sock for you that'll be perfect. You can sew a little piece of white circular fabric on it for the panda's belly. Maybe use a scrap of fabric for a little pink tongue."

"I'd like to make a zebra puppet with a hot pink mane," said Rachel. "I brought a black-and-white-striped sock that'll work for the body."

"Let's watch the instructions and then we can get started," Claire said, pressing play.

We all huddled around the laptop to watch the video. In it, a woman with short dark spiky hair and an Australian accent went through the sock puppet monkey process step by step. Here's what she told us to do:

1. Choose your sock.
2. Gather your supplies. A needle, thread, glue, fabric and buttons and beads and sequins to use as eyes, noses, and mouths, more fabric for clothes if you choose to clothe your doll, and stuffing if you choose to stuff.
3. Get to work decorating your puppet!
4. Enjoy!

Everything seemed pretty straightforward, and there was nothing stopping us. We had glue. We had googly eyes and tons of yarn in a gazillion different colors and glitter and sequins and fabric scraps. We had lots of creativity and imagination and motivation and time.

We sat down at the table.

I dumped all my old socks out of my backpack, and Rachel and Emma did the same. Claire's were already there in a pile with the rest of the supplies.

"I can't believe you all took her seriously!" said Yumi. "Now I feel ridiculous."

Claire handed her a tube sock with red and blue stripes. "Don't worry about it. You can start with this."

"And we can all share," I added.

"Thanks," said Yumi.

I picked out a fuzzy, green-and-blue-and-yellow-striped sock and got to work. We all did, sewing in silence, each of us focused on making the cutest sock puppet monkey possible. I wasn't so crafty in my regular life, but I had to admit, this was fun. Ten minutes later we were all just about finished with our first puppets.

"Check this out!" said Claire, holding up her doll. It was wild and colorful, with one green eye and one blue eye and a miniature black leather jacket and a mop of shaggy blue hair.

"Wow, that looks like it belongs on the cover of *Vogue*," said Emma. "I love it."

"What did you make?" Claire asked.

Emma held up an owl with glasses and a little peach-colored frock.

"She kind of looks like you," Claire said.

"Hoo!" Emma chirped in her best owl voice.

"She means the doll," said Yumi.

"Hoo!" Emma said again, smiling.

"Oh, you're making owl noises," I said. "I get it."

Everyone giggled.

"It's funny how all our dolls say so much about us," said Yumi as she tried to fashion a baseball cap out of a tiny piece of blue fabric.

"Are all your puppets going to be Dodgers themed?" asked Claire.

"No, I think I'm going to make a tennis player next," said Yumi.

"My puppet has frizzy hair just like me," said Rachel, holding up her puppet, which also featured a ski cap in the exact same color as Rachel's.

We all cracked up.

"You need to add freckles and it'll be perfect," said Emma.

Rachel considered her puppet. "Good point. Hey, Claire. What should I use for freckles?"

Claire handed her a brown Magic Marker. "This one's got an extra-fine point."

"Thanks. That's perfect!" Rachel said with a smile, uncapping it and dotting her doll's cheeks and the bridge of her nose. "Now I have my own mini-me!"

"What did you make, Annabelle?" asked Yumi.

I held up my own puppet, which was a puppy like Pepper—black-and-white and holding a bone in his mouth.

"These are all so cute!" Claire exclaimed. "We're totally going to clean up!"

I stuffed my puppet with cotton and sewed up the bottom and then fashioned his legs, tying off bits of the bottom with rubber bands, just like the lady had demonstrated on the YouTube video.

After that, I made a jogging puppet with fluorescent running shorts and a white tank top.

"Is that supposed to be your stepdad?" asked Claire.

"Sure," I said. "I didn't even realize it while I was making it, but yeah, Ted runs every morning in crazy clothes like these."

An hour later one of Claire's moms, Mollie, came home. "You girls are all so quiet, I didn't even know anyone was home," she said, giving Claire a hug as she surveyed our work.

"That's because we're creating masterpieces," said Claire. She held up her latest doll.

It was spectacular—with a pink fuzzy body and green googly eyes, and bright blue shaggy hair and a tail made of braided red yarn.

"I love it!" I said. "But what is it?"

"It's the cutest rat you've ever seen," Claire declared.

"I would totally buy that," said Yumi.

"Awesome-sauce. That's the point!" said Claire.

"In fact, I'd like to buy it for my little sister," said Yumi.

Claire tossed it into the pile of finished sock puppets. "You've gotta wait until tomorrow."

"These are all incredible," Mollie marveled.

I wasn't normally one to brag, but I had to agree—the monkeys were amazing-looking. "These totally look like they belong in a toy store," I said.

"Agreed," Rachel nodded as she checked her phone. "Uh-oh. My mom just texted me that I have to be home for dinner."

I glanced at the window and noticed that the sun was going down. "Oh, me too. I didn't realize how late it was."

"Wait, before we go, we need to figure out a game plan," said Emma. "Like what should we charge?"

"Twenty bucks a puppet!" said Claire.

"I think that may be a bit steep," said Emma. "I mean, I know they're worth that, but we are dealing with middle-schoolers. And our country is still in a recession."

"How about six dollars each?" I asked.

"That sounds good to me," said Yumi, staring at the elephant she'd just finished making. "I'd totally pay six bucks for this."

"I think that sounds fair too," said Emma.

"Okay," said Claire. "So are we bringing these to school tomorrow or should we wait until we have more inventory?"

"Let's start tomorrow!" said Emma. "I can't wait!"

"Yeah, it'll be good to know if people actually want these so we don't have to waste time making a ton," said Rachel.

"Of course people are going to want them," said Claire. "They're adorable!"

"I like the idea of having a small number to sell at first," said Emma. "That way, they're exclusive. Everyone is going to want one, and not everyone can have one. It'll drive up demand, get people really excited."

"Wait, before we go, I was thinking. Maybe we should name each of the monkeys?" asked Claire.

"Yes, let's definitely name them. Great idea!" said Emma. "That way everyone will know they're one-of-a-kind designer sock puppets."

"This one is Seymour," I said, holding up my latest creation. "Because he's wearing glasses. Get it? He can see more?"

"Hardy har har," said Emma.

"What if we stitch their names on their backs?" asked Claire. "It'll be like a tattoo!"

Emma nodded. "Or like a fashion label."

"What's yours going to be named?" Yumi asked.

"Alastair," said Emma, holding her latest puppet up to her cheek. "Because he's so sophisticated."

"Mine is named Geoffrey. With a 'G' not a 'J.' You know, because it's classier," said Rachel.

"Hey, how come they're all guys?" asked Yumi. "I'm naming mine Beatrix."

"After Beatrix Potter?" I asked.

"No, just plain Beatrix. She is her own sock puppet."

Claire gave us some embroidery needles and we got to work.

I chose purple string to start with, and even simply threading the needle was tricky. "This is hard," I said, squinting at my work. "I think I'm going to change the name of my sock to TJ. It's much easier to stitch out."

After I gave my puppets initials, I said good-bye to my friends and packed up my stuff.

I was so inspired by the new sock puppet monkey idea that as soon as I finished my dinner, I went back upstairs and cleaned out my sock drawer.

A minute later Ted came in so he could finish transferring my contacts to my new phone. As soon as he handed it to me, it rang. Oliver's name flashed on the screen, and I felt my heart get all melty.

"Hello?" I said, hoping I didn't sound too giddy.

"It's Oliver," said Oliver.

"Yeah—I know! Your name shows up on my screen."

"Oh, right. I forgot. Um, where've you been?" he asked.

"At Claire's. We came up with the best new business plan."

I glanced at Ted and luckily he knew to leave the room. Then I told Oliver all about the sock puppets.

"I remember those," Oliver said. "My brother and I made a bunch a few years ago. I think I still have one somewhere in the attic."

"You should find it," I said. "Because pretty soon they're going to be in demand."

He laughed.

"Wait," I said. "On second thought, don't find it. It'll be much better for me if you buy a new one!"

We compared answers on our math homework because even though we're not in the same class, we have the same teacher. And after I hung up, I went downstairs and showed off TJ to my mom and Ted.

"Oh, he's adorable," said my mom.

"Thanks," I replied, proudly.

"I agree—very cute," said Ted. "And I think your plan is brilliant. I'm so proud of you girls, and I wish you all the success in the world."

"Thanks," I said. "But I can't really take any credit. It was all Claire's idea."

"But you made this, right?" asked Ted, inspecting TJ.

"Yup," I said. "And that's my old sock, too."

"I hope you washed it first," said Ted, holding it away and making a face.

"It's definitely clean," I assured him, giggling as I took the sock puppet back.

"I'd like to be your first customer," said my mom. "I'm sure your new baby brother or sister would love this."

I bit my bottom lip and thought for a moment. "We're supposed to wait until tomorrow at lunch," I said. "But I suppose I can make an exception. You know—since you're family, and all."

My mom grinned. "I appreciate that. How much is it?"

I started to say six dollars but stopped myself because I had an idea. This could be a great opportunity. "Well, that one is special," I said. "It'll be one thousand dollars."

My mom laughed, figuring I was kidding. And I was, but I kept a straight face.

"One thousand dollars for one sock puppet?" she asked. "Isn't that a bit, um, much?"

"Well, yes," I said. "But think. All we need to do is sell one and we're totally set!"

chapter thirteen
sock puppets to the rescue

I left my house early and walked to school faster than usual. I was so excited, it was hard to keep from running. This was a really big morning. Once on campus I noticed other kids moving sleepily, dragging their feet and yawning, but not me and my friends. We were all on high alert, standing at our locker banks at the ready. Emma especially looked poised for some serious business dealings.

"Is that a suit jacket?" Yumi asked her.

Emma brushed some imaginary dust off the shoulder of her navy-blue blazer. "This is part of my debate team uniform," she said. "I'm wearing it for good luck. And because you know, you've gotta dress for success."

"It's a little preppy for my taste," said Claire. "But I respect your philosophy."

"Thanks," said Emma. "Now let's get to work. I've figured out the perfect plan, and here's what we're going to do. First we need to go to the busiest place at school. Then, Annabelle, you show Claire the sock puppet monkey and Claire, you pretend like you're seeing it for the very first time. Act impressed and make sure you're super-loud and enthusiastic about it. You know—to attract a lot of attention."

"I'll act like I'm seeing the greatest thing ever invented," said Claire.

"Perfect!" said Emma.

"What, that's your big plan?" asked Rachel, always the skeptical one.

"Yeah, we're gonna create buzz—it's called viral marketing, and it's going to work," Emma explained. Then she turned to me and said, "You, too, Annabelle. Be sure to keep up the energy!"

"Got it," I said, giving her a double thumbs-up.

We all headed over to the main quad. Our timing was perfect. This was total Birchwood Middle School rush hour.

I positioned myself between three large crowds of kids, and pulled TJ out of my backpack. He looked even cuter than he did last night! "So, check this out," I said to Claire, shouting over the noise and holding TJ up high over my head. "Isn't this the most adorable thing you've ever seen in your entire life?"

"Omigosh!" Claire exclaimed, even louder. "That is awesome. I love sock puppets! Where'd you get it?"

"Some girl named Emma sold it to me!" I yelled. "And, apparently, there are a bunch more that are just as cute—maybe cuter. They'll all be available at lunchtime."

From the corner of my eye, I noticed a few kids watching us.

"It's seriously the cutest thing I have ever seen!" Claire bellowed. "I must have one, immediately!"

Just then Yumi walked by. Claire yelled to her, "Hey, check this out!"

"What is it?" asked Yumi.

"A sock puppet!" I exclaimed, going through the entire explanation all over again—even louder this time.

"That is awesome! I totally need one!" Yumi yelled.

This crazy plan seemed to be working. We were definitely making a big scene, and plenty of kids turned their heads. They were intrigued—I could tell. So I went on. "They're all handmade, too. From organic cotton."

Claire looked at me quizzically with one raised eyebrow, and we both had to struggle to keep from laughing. Okay, I kind of made up the part about the socks being organic, probably because I was around so much organic cotton these days—what with my mom and Ted getting ready for the new baby.

Luckily, though, Claire recovered from her surprise quickly. "I love organic sock puppets!" she exclaimed.

I was super-impressed with her performance. Every time I thought she'd reached her peak of enthusiasm, she outdid herself.

"Me too!" Yumi shouted. Both of them were now jumping up and down and holding hands, like they'd just found out Katy Perry was their substitute teacher for the day.

A crowd formed around us and people seemed to be whispering to one another, wondering what was up. I struggled to keep from cracking up at the absurdity of it all. Emma's crazy plan was working! I felt like we were all characters in a really funny play.

I wanted to start selling the puppets immediately, but the first bell rang before I could ask Emma to break out our supply, so I stuffed my puppet into my backpack and ran to homeroom.

The morning seemed to last forever, and yet I couldn't recall a thing I learned in class. Other than the fact that I didn't want to be there! I was too excited about lunch. Nervous, too. What if we couldn't sell enough sock puppets? What if we couldn't sell any? What if people laughed at our efforts? Sure, my friends and I thought our sock puppets were spectacular works of art, but what if we were all fooling ourselves because we wanted so badly to go to the Panda Parade?

The suspense was driving me bonkers. I seriously felt ready to burst with anticipation, like if lunchtime didn't happen soon, I would spontaneously combust.

And then, when lunch *finally* arrived, things got super-crazy. Here was how it all went down: we sat down at our regular table and lined up all the sock puppets. They looked even better than they had last night! The entire display was awesome and people noticed.

Oliver was the first kid to walk over, although that was no great shocker. My boyfriend was a plant. Not a fern or a rhododendron or a stick of bamboo. I mean, I'd texted him a script right after first period, with instructions to memorize his lines and deliver them at lunch. And, luckily, he was totally game, not to mention a really, really good actor.

"Hey, what are these?" Oliver asked, sounding completely innocent.

"These are sock puppet monkeys," said Claire, holding up one of the puppets as if it were a fancy diamond necklace and she was a fancy spokesperson on QVC, offering him an exclusive and limited one-time offer. "Handmade, one-of-a-kind objects of art." She cradled the puppet in one hand and used the other to sweep over it in flourishes, like a magician.

"What are you doing with them?" he asked, looking back and forth between us.

Claire was still wiggling her fingers around the puppets, and now Rachel had joined in too, waving both hands like a hula dancer at a luau.

Yumi giggled, but I did my best to ignore her.

"Selling them," I said, all business, handing him a turtle I'd made out of an old green sock. It had blue eyes and a brown plaid shell. I was particularly excited about the plaid—each little diamond shape had been carefully stitched with a color of embroidery thread called burnt sunset, which was a fancy term for orange.

"This is so cute," said Oliver.

His sparkly eyes crinkled in the corners when he smiled in the most adorable way, but I couldn't let that distract me. I had a job to do!

"Want to buy it?" I asked. "His name is Mr. Wright and he costs six dollars."

"And the money goes to a good cause," said Emma. "It'll help save the endangered pandas."

"And it'll help promote our contemporary music education," Yumi added.

I had to stifle a laugh. That sounded so much better than saying we needed to raise money so we could go to a concert. And I guess it was technically still true.

"Well, how can I say no?" asked Oliver, gallantly pulling his wallet from his back pocket.

"You can't," I said, grinning as I took the crumpled bills from him. "Thank you for the exact change."

"No problem!" said Oliver. "I learned my lesson at the lemonade stand. No IOUs allowed."

"That's right," said Emma, taking the money from me and putting it in our cash box, since she was the official treasurer.

Oliver took Charlie and walked him back over to his side of the cafeteria.

And moments later we had an actual audience of real kids who were genuinely interested in our sock puppets. Hannah moved in closer and so did Lennon and Eddie, who are in my gym class. Maddy and CJ from French class seemed intrigued too. Taylor and

Nikki watched suspiciously from their regular table, eyes narrowed and arms crossed over their chests. But that was kind of how they watched everything. I didn't really care if they thought our sock puppets were dumb. The point was—they'd noticed them. And that was good enough.

Since no one else was actually approaching us, I waved Hannah over, calling, "Hey, come check out what we made."

"Are these the sock puppets that everyone's been talking about?" she asked, walking closer.

"Everyone's been talking about them?" Claire asked, amazed.

Emma elbowed her. "Of course they have and these are them."

Hannah picked up one of Yumi's Dodgers dogs. "You really put this all together yourself?" she asked.

"We did," said Yumi. "Want to buy it?"

"My little cousin is coming to town this weekend, and he's the biggest Dodgers fan in the world. He'd love this!'

"Awesome!" I said.

Hannah pulled some crumpled bills out of the front pocket of her shorts and also counted out a dollar in quarters and handed it all over. As she walked away with her sock puppet, I noticed all the boys who sit at the other end of our lunch table watch. They'd been ignoring us up until a minute ago, but now Corn

Dog Joe set down his corn dog and slid across the bench seat so he was closer.

"What are those things?" he asked, his brown eyes darting back and forth between me and our display.

Claire went through the entire explanation again— loudly—really focusing on the handmade elements and how carefully each doll had been constructed. And before we knew it, a small crowd had gathered around.

Joe bought a blue elephant puppet, and as soon as he left, three more kids came over.

Everyone wanted to know about our sock puppets. And better yet—lots of kids were pulling out their wallets, digging for change in their backpacks, and pooling their money so they could go in on a sock puppet together.

It was wild.

By the time the lunch bell rang, we'd sold out.

We didn't have time to count all the cash, but I knew we had each made three monkeys and there were five of us, which means we'd sold fifteen. At six dollars each, that meant we'd made ninety dollars. In other words, in forty-five minutes we'd sold enough monkeys for almost one ticket to the Panda Parade.

"This is crazy," I said to Emma as she placed the money in our cash box and locked it. "If we have another six lunches like this, we'll be set!"

"I know," she whispered, her eyes bright with excitement.

"Emergency crafting session at my place tonight!" Claire yelled, throwing her arms over her head in a victory stance.

"You've been waiting all your life to use the phrase, 'emergency crafting session,' haven't you?" asked Yumi.

"You know me too well," Claire replied, putting her arm around Yumi and giving her a squeeze. "See y'all later!"

We parted ways, and I headed to science. But on my way there I noticed something distressing. Oliver and Tobias were throwing Charlie the turtle back and forth across the breezeway like a football.

"Hey, what are you doing to Charlie?" I called.

"These are really aerodynamic," said Oliver. "Look at how far he goes."

Oliver tossed him again before I could protest. And then I noticed something else fly by in my peripheral vision.

Apparently, another kid with a zebra decided to throw her sock puppet too. Except no one was there to catch the poor thing—Zinnea, I think her name was. She landed even farther in the grass, facedown, her hot-pink mane ruffled. Seeing Zinnea splayed out on the lawn got me a little upset, even though she's just a sock puppet.

I bent down and picked her up, brushing the grass off her nuzzle.

"Hey, that's mine!" yelled a skinny girl with braids and glasses.

"Sorry, but she wasn't really designed to be used like a football," I said, handing it back to the girl.

"I actually tossed her like a softball," said the girl before hurrying away, her sock puppet tucked in close to her chest.

"Come on, Annabelle," Oliver said with a laugh. "Be a good sport."

"We worked hard on those," I protested.

"And I totally appreciate it," said Oliver. "This is better than my Nerf football."

"Yo, toss it over here," Tobias called. "I'm wide open."

"Of course you are," I said. "You're the only two playing this ridiculous game!"

Oliver ignored me, faked right, and then threw his turtle to the left. Tobias caught it and brought it in close to his body and charged through the hall with one arm out.

I shook my head and tried to laugh it off as I walked to class.

On my way there I noticed the pink elephant I'd made sticking out of someone's backpack. It was a person I didn't even know. I think she was an eighth-grader or she was at least tall enough to be one. I couldn't believe even eighth-graders wanted these things. The plan was working out better than I'd imagined.

After school we went to Claire's where we confirmed that we'd made ninety dollars.

"This is so super-fantastic!" I said.

"I know," said Emma. "But it also means we need to start working even harder. I've gotten text messages from five different people asking us when we're going to have more sock puppets. These things are trending big time, which is why we've got to strike now—keep up the supply while the demand is still great. Things can change in a flash." She snapped her fingers.

"Wait, did you just demonstrate how fast a flash actually is?" asked Claire with a laugh. She snapped herself. "Is that the scientific definition? *Snap!*"

"Don't make fun," said Emma, sticking her tongue out at Claire. "This is serious stuff. Right now we're on a rocket ship and we've got to keep up."

"If we're on the rocket ship, won't it carry us along with it?" asked Claire.

"You know what I mean," Emma said. "We need to double our inventory. Selling out is great, but we only had fifteen puppets. I'd like to show up to lunch tomorrow with twice that many."

"So let's get started!" I said.

Pretty soon we were up to our elbows in yarn and sequins and googly eyes and socks.

We listened to the new Katy Perry album from Claire's computer, heads bent over our sewing. And for the first time in a while I felt hopeful about the Panda Parade—as opposed to scared that we wouldn't be able to raise the cash in time.

"I love how we're all working like there's no tomorrow," said Claire.

"That expression actually makes no sense whatsoever," said Emma. "We're working like there is a tomorrow—a tomorrow where our sock puppets are going to be in huge demand."

"Lucky for us," I said.

"I can't believe we had to suffer through two failed businesses for this," said Rachel.

"You know what they say," said Emma as she glued an eye onto her aardvark puppet. "Third time's a charm."

We worked in silence for a while, and I was happy to see that the next few puppets came easily to me. I made a baby lion with an orange-and-yellow mane, an elephant wearing a red jumper, and a dalmatian puppy.

An hour later Claire's mom Mollie came into the dining room and said, "You girls are working so hard! If it's okay with your parents, may I take you all out to dinner?"

"We really shouldn't stop," said Emma. "We've got a lot of work to do."

"But we can't sew on an empty stomach," said Rachel. "I'm going to text my mom and ask for permission."

"Good idea. Me too," I said as I pulled out my phone.

"You got an iPhone!" said Rachel. Except from the harsh tone of her voice, she sounded more like she was accusing me of something horrible.

I felt a sinking feeling in my stomach. This was the exact conversation I was hoping to avoid—I didn't even realize that I'd been hiding my new phone from her since I got it. But I kind of had been—subconsciously, I suppose.

"It's not new. It's actually pretty old. Ted gave me his old one when he upgraded to the latest model."

Rachel looked down at her phone and sort of pouted as she said, "Of course he did."

I didn't say anything as I texted my mom, but I was plenty annoyed. I knew what Rachel was thinking and it wasn't fair. Why'd she have to make me feel bad for every new thing I got? And why'd she have to ruin our perfectly good afternoon?

I didn't ask her any of this out loud because I didn't want to fight. Instead I tried to pretend she'd never even said a word about my phone. That's how everyone else was acting.

Once we had all gotten permission, we piled into Claire's mom's minivan. I sat as far from Rachel as possible. Both of us stayed pretty quiet while the rest of our friends chatted on the drive over to the Round Table.

As we walked toward the restaurant, we passed by a toy store called Play Matters. The window displayed tons of cool-looking toys—a fancy wooden train track, some robots, and a bunch of vintage-looking toy airplanes.

"Oh, I used to love that place," said Claire. "My grandma would take me there whenever she visited."

Emma paused in front of the store and stared into the window. "Mine too. Hey, I just had an idea," she said, heading into the store and calling, "I'll be right back."

We all watched through the window as she took a puppet out of her backpack and showed it to the woman working behind the counter. They talked for a while, and then a few minutes later Emma came out with a huge smile on her face.

"What's that about?" I asked.

"Play Matters has agreed to sell our puppets!"

"No way!" I said.

"Way!" Emma replied. "The manager said she liked my spirit and enthusiasm, so she's agreed to take five of them to see how they do."

"That's, like, a real store!" Yumi said.

"It sure is," said Emma.

Claire raised her hand. "High five!"

"Panda Parade here we come!" Yumi cheered.

chapter fourteen
crafting emergencies

The sock puppet sale scene on Friday was even more frenzied than on day one. Word had definitely gotten out, and we sold our entire supply before the first homeroom bell. By lunchtime, kids were clamoring for more sock puppets.

"When are you going to have more?" asked Isabel from my English class.

"Monday morning," said Claire.

"Okay, but how can you make sure I get a bunch before they sell out?" asked Hannah. Her cousin loved the sock puppet so much, apparently, he'd asked for three more so he could have a whole sock puppet family.

"We can't," said Emma. "You've gotta make sure you beat the crowd."

"This is so super-stressful!" said Hannah.

"I'll save you a few," I whispered to her. "Just don't tell anyone else."

Hannah gave me a thumbs-up and walked away.

Meanwhile a few seventh graders made their way

over to our table and asked if we were the geniuses behind the sock puppets.

"Yup," said Claire. "And these geniuses need to eat lunch. We'll have a bunch more next week. Promise."

The rest of us giggled as the seventh-graders walked away.

"You guys, this is crazy!" said Emma.

"Crazy brilliant," said Claire.

We had yet another crafting session in Claire's dining room that afternoon. And the next day too. And after that we ran out of supplies, so we had to hit the art supply store for more bling, as well as the department store for more socks. Luckily, Claire's mom was available to drive us to the mall first thing Sunday morning.

"Don't we have enough money for tickets yet?" Rachel asked as we piled into the minivan. "We've sold more than a hundred puppets, right?"

"Yeah," said Emma. "So that makes six hundred dollars of pure profit, but now we've got to reinvest and spend money on supplies so we can keep things up."

"Just make sure we don't spend too much," said Rachel.

"I won't," said Emma, opening up her notebook to do some math equations. "I already figured things out. If we spend an average of two dollars and fifty cents on materials, that means our profit is three dollars and fifty cents per puppet, which is still pretty awesome. All we need is for the next two weeks to be good as last week."

Just then Emma looked down at her ringing cell phone. "Hold on a second. I've gotta take this call."

Claire looked at me with raised eyebrows, and I shrugged. Then we eavesdropped on Emma's end of the conversation.

"Okay, you want three monkeys and six more dogs and another rabbit? Just one? Any color preferences?" Emma asked, cradling her phone between her head and her shoulder as she jotted down some notes in her notebook.

After she hung up she retied her ponytail. "These orders are really stacking up."

"That's cool," said Claire. "But when did we agree to do custom puppets?"

Emma frowned at Claire. "We didn't, exactly, but these are for Play Matters, the toy store by the pizza place."

"I remember," said Claire. "Are you telling me they sold out?"

"Yup," said Emma. "And now they want twenty more for their window display."

"But that'll take us hours," said Yumi. "How are we going to do that and make enough puppets for school?"

"We'll figure it out," I said. "We have all weekend."

"And here we are," Claire added as her mom pulled up to the entrance to the mall.

"Is an hour enough time for you girls?" Mollie asked.

"Should be," said Claire.

"I'll meet you all right here by these front doors. Claire, keep your phone on. I will be calling if you're late."

"Got it!" said Claire, saluting her mom.

"And stick together!" Mollie added.

The five of us climbed out of the van and hit Zingerman's Art Supplies first. I'd never been, and walking into the store was a shock in the best possible sense.

"I've never seen so much color in one place," I said as Yumi took a shopping cart.

"I know," said Claire, grabbing my hand. "Come with me. I want to show you my favorite aisle."

We all jogged to keep up and ended up surrounded by more sequins than I knew existed in the state of California.

"There are ten different shades of green sparkly sequins," said Claire. "And I want every single one!"

"Look, Dodger Blue is actually the official name of this shade," said Yumi, excitedly throwing some paint into our cart.

"Don't forget the puffy paint," said Rachel, throwing in an entire set.

Claire settled on five shades of green and we got plenty of other sequins too. And buttons and random scraps of fabric and yarn, and we even sprung for a glue gun.

When we got to the cash register, we were shocked at the total. Everything added up to more than a hundred dollars.

"Are you sure we should spend this much?" Rachel whispered to Emma.

Emma shrugged. "You've got to spend money to make money, right?"

She handed over the cash and then we hit Target to load up on socks.

As amazing as I thought our first few batches of sock puppets were, I had to admit the ones that came later were truly spectacular. There was Raymond, the purple monkey with electric blue eyes; Chantelle, the poodle with rainbow bows on her ears; and Cobalt, a construction worker who tied his long black curls back with a red bandanna.

Two weeks into our launch, kids at Birchwood Middle School were still crazy for our sock puppets. Some days we brought ten to school and some days we brought twenty. On Friday, one of our nautical-themed sailor puppets lost an eye in transit. It didn't matter—we still sold out!

We spent another Saturday stocking up on supplies and then crafting.

At some point I lost count of how many sock puppets we'd all made. It seemed like hundreds. Everyone we knew had at least one. And people wanted more.

"Can we really still call these emergency crafting

sessions?" asked Claire. "Considering that we seem to have one every single day."

"You make a really good point," said Emma.

"I think we need an emergency vacation day," said Rachel.

"We're taking the day off for my birthday this weekend, right?" I asked.

"Omigosh, I can't believe you're finally turning twelve," said Yumi.

"Don't worry, Annabelle. We won't be crafting next Saturday. It's in the schedule."

I laughed. "Glad you could fit my birthday into your busy schedule."

"So am I!" Emma replied, totally serious.

Claire threw a fluffy teddy-bear-in-a-clown-suit sock puppet at her. "She was being sarcastic."

"Oh," said Emma. "Right. I totally knew that. I was just joking."

"Way to make me feel special on my birthday," I said.

"Hey, it's not your birthday yet," Emma reminded me.

"I'm glad it's soon," said Yumi. "I definitely need a day off."

"I know," I said. "I used to look forward to getting out of school, but lately I dread it because there's so much work to be done."

"Every time I think about sock puppets, my hands hurt," said Rachel.

"My back aches from being hunched over all the time," said Yumi. "We must have enough money for the tickets by now. Right, Emma?"

"Not quite," said Emma.

"Well, we must be close at least," said Rachel.

"I hope so," said Claire. "Because just looking at this pile of fabric scraps is making me sick. I'm so ready to retire."

"When can we buy our concert tickets?" asked Yumi. "Every time we ask, you avoid the question."

This was true. Emma had been keeping careful records of each puppet and each sale from the moment we launched our business. She had an entire notebook devoted to the project, but she wouldn't show us what was inside. "I want to really wow you guys, and I'm waiting for the right time," Emma said.

The rest of us stopped what we were doing and looked up at her.

"I think now is the right time," said Claire.

"I agree," said Rachel.

Emma sighed and opened up her notebook, flipping to the right page.

"We're definitely close but we're not there yet. The problem is every time we buy new supplies, we end up spending more money. But if we make the stuff we have last, we'll only need to make and sell fifteen more puppets for the tickets and travel expenses," said Emma.

"That's nothing!" said Claire. "We can do that tomorrow."

"Wait," said Emma. "There's a better option. If we sell forty more, we'll have enough cash for T-shirts, too."

"We've never sold forty," said Claire. "It makes me nervous. I don't even know forty kids who don't already have our puppets."

"People are doubling up," said Yumi.

"But do you think they'll triple up?"

"I don't see why not," said Emma. "And I've been thinking about strategy. Do you remember when the last iPad came out, how there was a big shortage and people were lining up for hours at the Apple store hoping to get one? And there were wait lists and everything?"

"Totally," I said. "Ted had to order his from Wisconsin and pay extra to have it rush delivered."

As soon as I said this, I wished I could take it back. I glanced at Rachel out of the corner of my eye. She seemed to be rolling her eyes, but I wasn't positive. Maybe it was my imagination. I hoped so. I was so sick of her making rude comments, I'd been going out of my way not to say anything that could even be misconstrued as me being braggy or whatever.

Luckily, she didn't say a word or even look at me.

Claire chimed in instead. "So they didn't manufacture enough?" she asked. "What does that have to do with us?"

"They didn't make enough on purpose," said Emma. "By making the iPad hard to get and exclusive, more people wanted it. And it totally paid off. So I was thinking, maybe we should *not* sell sock puppets for a few days and really build demand, create a panic in the marketplace."

"What if people forget about them?" asked Rachel.

"Yeah, remember when everyone was into Rainbow Loom and then winter break happened and when we got back, no one cared?" Yumi said.

"Not only that, people started making fun of kids who were still wearing their Rainbow Loom jewelry," I said.

Emma shook her head. "That won't happen to our sock puppets."

"Are you sure?" asked Claire.

"Winter break was for three weeks. I'm just saying we take five days off," said Emma. "That way we can stop what we're doing now, enjoy the week, and get back to work next weekend."

"Not Saturday," I said. "That's my birthday."

"Sunday then," said Emma. "We can have a marathon session. Make eight puppets each and really make them count."

"It would be nice to have a break," said Claire. "What does everyone else think?"

"Let's vote on it," I said.

"All in favor of taking a week off, raise your hand," said Emma.

She raised her hand and then Rachel raised hers and Yumi and Claire followed and I did too.

"It's unanimous," Emma said with a smile. "But are you guys agreeing with my strategy or just wanting to take a break?"

"I would say a little of both," said Claire. "But does it even matter?"

Emma slammed her notebook shut, stood up from the table, and stretched. "You guys, this is going to be amazing!"

My friends and I all agreed. It seemed like nothing could go wrong. But I guess those are famous last words for a reason.

chapter fifteen
unhappy birthday

You bought balloons?" I cried, coming downstairs first thing in the morning and finding—to my horror—that the entire living room was filled with silver and blue balloons. My mom and Ted had gotten the regular kind as well as a bunch of those shiny Mylar balloons that said HAPPY BIRTHDAY on them with streamers and firecracker-like bursts of confetti in all the colors of the rainbow.

"Surprise," said my mom, who was in the middle of putting up red and blue streamers. "I can't believe you're twelve."

"And I can't believe you bought me balloons without asking first," I said. "This is so not cool, Mom! Twelve-year-olds don't have balloons at their birthday parties!"

"They don't?" my mom asked.

Her reaction left me dumbfounded. How could she be so clueless? It made no sense!

"No!" I shouted.

I tried to think back to Emma's and Rachel's and Claire's and Yumi's parties. They had all been fun. But had it been balloon-type fun? I couldn't recall, but I didn't think so.

Of course, my party was different from theirs. I'd invited a few boys as well as my usual group of friends. And since this was my first boy-girl party, I was guessing that balloons were totally inappropriate.

"What's wrong with balloons?" Ted asked, coming into the living room.

"Only babies have balloons at their birthdays!" I cried.

My mom looked from me to the balloons. "I had balloons at my baby shower last week and they were lovely!"

"That totally proves my point," I exclaimed. "Those balloons weren't for you—they were because of the future baby."

Ted put his arm around my mom and said, "When I turned fifty last year, I had a hundred balloons at my party."

"I remember," said my mom. "That was such an amazing night—and the balloons were a wonderful addition."

Every time one of them said "balloon," I wanted to tear my hair out. Not literally, obviously, because the only thing worse than having a babyish balloon-themed party was attending said party bald. I mean, come on—things were already bad enough. "You guys are totally not getting it," I said. Okay, maybe I shouted. Probably, I did. But I couldn't help myself.

My mom and Ted just stared at me, like I'd been replaced by my bad-tempered alien clone. Like they didn't even know who I was and clearly, they didn't— hence the unauthorized balloon purchase. My gosh! As I stared at them, I realized how awful this was. The entire room would've been perfect for some kid turning six, but as of this morning I'm twice as old. This was a total disaster.

I took a deep breath and blinked hard and tried not to cry because I did not want red and puffy eyes for my party. Plus, crying would only reinforce my whole point—that balloons were babyish—and I was not going to act like a baby. But still. I was so angry. How could they buy balloons for me without asking? Ted, I could understand. He didn't know me that well, and he'd never had a daughter before. But my mom? She knew that this party was a very big deal. She knew that Oliver was going to be there and other boys, too: Sanjay, Tobias, Corn Dog Joe. We'd talked about the menu and the music and the cake and the whole swimming thing. She'd been so, so careful, asking my permission about everything. She definitely should've known better when it came to the balloons.

"Fine," I said, trying my best to be patient with them. "I guess balloons are okay for old people and they're okay for babies, but they are not okay for me."

"Annabelle, I think you're being a little silly about this," my mom said, waving at the balloons with both hands as if they were some kind of amazing thing. "They're festive and sophisticated. Balloons are perfect for all birthday parties. It doesn't matter how old you are. Now, I know you're nervous about the party, but—"

"I am *not* nervous about the party!" I shouted. "Why would you even say that? And how come you sound like some public service announcement for balloons?"

"Tell you what," said Ted, clapping his hands once. "I'll gather up all the balloons and put them in a closet. If you decide you want them later on, you can have them. If not, it's no big deal. Obviously, we should've checked with you first, Annabelle. It's your birthday."

"Just make sure they're in a closet far away from the party space," I said.

"That's enough, Annabelle!" my mom snapped.

"It's fine," said Ted holding up his hands in surrender. "I'll put them upstairs in my closet. Okay?"

"Thank you!" I huffed, turning around and storming out of the room. Okay, part of me felt bratty for acting this way, but honestly, I couldn't help myself.

My mom started to go after me, but then I overheard Ted say, "Honey, wait. Give her some space." And she listened to him—thankfully!

My mom was acting so weird these days, and

I figured it was because she was pregnant or maybe just so focused on the new baby that she was forgetting that she had a teenager now.

Okay, turning twelve did not make me an official teenager, but it sure put me close. I was merely a year away from being thirteen, which was a very big deal.

As soon as I got upstairs I opened up my closet and began shifting through my wardrobe. I was acutely aware of the fact that I only got to turn twelve once, and I didn't want to mess things up.

I'd just gotten a new bathing suit for the pool party. It was a blue-and-purple paisley tankini. I knew Rachel was going to say something about my new suit and I didn't want to have to answer to her. Deep down I had to admit to myself that I didn't even want her at the party at all. I felt bad about that, but it was true. Rachel had changed. She was not the same girl she used to be. But would she ever go back to the way she used to be, or was this the new Rachel? And if this was the new Rachel, did I want to spend so much time with her? Did I even want her to be my friend?

People grow up and grow apart—it's a fact of life. That's what people say, anyway. So it must be true. Right?

This year had already been a time of crazy change. I thought about my last birthday—turning eleven had seemed like a big deal too. I was still in my old apartment. I'd gone to a different school in a different town and had different friends. Mia and Sophia were my best friends then, but now I hardly spoke to them. I'd invited them to the party today, even though I hadn't seen them in months, but it turns out they were busy. They had a dance recital at Ballerina Suprema—the dance studio where we all used to take classes. I actually never liked ballet so much—I danced because my best friends did. I was glad I was having a big pool party instead of being in a dance recital. I never liked the costumes, either—they always itched. And being onstage—it was a lot of pressure. Not fun.

I put on the new tankini and then slathered on sunscreen because I knew my mom would ask me about it. I had to prove that I was old and responsible enough—she didn't have to remind me about every small thing. Then I threw on a pair of cutoff jeans shorts and a red-and-blue-checked sleeveless, button-down shirt.

When I checked the clock, I realized my friends weren't due to arrive for thirty more minutes.

I looked around my room. Everyone might come up here at some point—even the boys—so I put the Uglydolls in the closet because even though they were cute and everything, I was twelve, which was probably too old for dolls of any kind.

I checked downstairs to make sure that the balloons were put away and they were. My mom and Ted had taken down the streamers, too. The room looked almost normal. Outside on the patio there was a giant bowl of watermelon, a jug of lemonade, and some chips and salsa. Also, a stack of plates and cups filled with spoons, forks, and knives, and napkins held under a rock, so they wouldn't blow away in the breeze.

It didn't look like a birthday party scene—just a regular party and that seemed cool. I grabbed my phone and took a few pictures.

"Everything meet with your approval?" asked Ted.

I spun around, surprised and a little embarrassed. "Yeah. It's great."

"Are you going to do a before-and-after thing?" asked Ted.

I smiled. "I don't know. I hadn't thought that far ahead. Um, thanks for handling the balloons. I don't know why my mom was being so difficult about them!"

Ted just smiled. He knew better than to take sides, I guess. "We're doing hamburgers and dogs, and veggie dogs for your vegetarian friends. Is that right?"

"Yup," I said with a nod. "Claire is the only vegetarian, but Emma might eat veggie dogs too because she likes them better."

"Got it." Ted saluted and went back inside. Then I took some more pictures and flattened out the tablecloth in the corner where it was wrinkled. Once I was sure everything looked perfect—and every trace of a balloon had vanished—I went back upstairs and tried to read.

I only got a few pages into my book when the doorbell rang.

I saw Ted heading for the door, but I raced downstairs to get there first. "I'll get it," I called.

"Okay." Ted turned around and went back into the kitchen.

Claire arrived first, carrying a gigantic blue box with a yellow ribbon. Also attached to the box were three helium balloons. "Happy Birthday, Annabelle!" she said, handing me the present.

I wondered if maybe I did overreact with the whole balloon thing. But a few balloons from my friend were very different from a room filled with balloons from my parents.

"Thanks, Claire," I said, giving her a hug. "But I said you didn't have to get me anything. I mean, come on, what can top these custom-made high-tops?" I asked, pointing to my feet.

"It's your birthday," said Claire as she walked inside. "I had to get you a gift and I wanted to too."

"Okay, thanks," I said. "I'm not going to complain!"

"Do you have your bathing suit on yet?" Claire wondered. "I wasn't sure if I should wear mine under my clothes or not."

"I do," I said.

"Oh, then let me run upstairs and change," said Claire.

I started to follow her to my room but then heard a knock at the door so I turned around again.

Oliver, Tobias, and Corn Dog Joe had all arrived together.

"Hi, guys," I said.

"Happy Birthday, Spazabelle," said Tobias.

"Hey, haven't we been over this a million times?" said Oliver, hitting Tobias on the back of his head.

"Sorry, dude," said Tobias. "I'm only kidding." He handed me a silver gift bag and gave me a stiff hug. "Thanks for inviting me over."

"No problem," I said.

"My mom made me promise to say that," Tobias said.

I laughed. "Yeah, I didn't think it came from you, spontaneously."

"So where's your pool?" asked Corn Dog Joe.

"Out back, dummy," said Tobias, shoving Corn Dog Joe.

"Hi, boys," Ted said, suddenly appearing in the entryway. "I'm Ted, Annabelle's stepdad. I know you, Oliver, but would you introduce me to these other fine gentlemen?"

"Um, sure," said Oliver, pointing to Tobias. "This is Tobias and this is Joe."

Ted held out his hand, and the boys shook it and murmured their "nice to meet you's." When Claire came hopping down the steps, two at a time, she said, "Hey, guys!"

"Now, does everyone know how to swim?" asked Ted.

"Of course they do!" I said.

Ted held up his hands in surrender. "Hey, it's my job as the responsible parent to ask."

"We can all swim, sir," said Oliver.

"Yeah, and no one's as fast as me," said Corn Dog Joe.

"Glad to hear it," Ted said.

Just then Pepper barked at the door, telling me Yumi and Emma had arrived. I let them in before they'd even knocked.

Now everyone was at my party except for one person. "Where's Rachel?" I asked.

Yumi and Emma exchanged a glance, like they shared a secret.

"What?" I asked.

"Nothing," Emma said with a cough. "Guess she'll be here later. You know how it is with her these days. She's always late."

"Let's swim!" said Yumi.

"Great idea," said Tobias.

I led everyone outside to the pool. I'd made an awesome mix on my iPhone, and my favorite Taylor Swift song blared from our new outdoor speakers.

The pool seemed even more inviting than usual, and the sun shined bright. It was perfect swim weather.

Life seemed pretty perfect. If I were to see this scene in a movie, I'd think, "That short, pale, blond girl is so lucky. She's got an awesome life."

"Last one in is a rotten egg!" yelled Oliver before peeling off his shirt, kicking off his flip-flops, and cannonballing in.

"You heard what the man said," Tobias said to Corn Dog Joe right before shoving him in.

I giggled as Corn Dog Joe surfaced.

"Dude, that is so not cool!" he yelled, taking off his T-shirt and throwing it at Tobias.

Tobias swerved to dodge the wet T-shirt, laughing the whole time. "It'll dry. What's the big deal?"

"You are so dead!" yelled Corn Dog Joe.

"Hey," said Oliver, treading water from the deep end. "I say Tobias has to do a belly flop to make up for that uncouth behavior."

"Totally!" I said.

"No way," said Tobias, pushing his bangs out of his eyes.

Corn Dog Joe cupped his hands over his mouth and began chanting, "Belly flop, belly flop, belly flop."

Oliver joined in and I did too. Then Claire and Emma and Yumi shouted, and pretty soon we were all chanting so loudly, I'm sure they could hear us down the street.

"Forget it!" Tobias said.

Oliver changed the chant to "Belly flop or go home," and we all picked up on that.

Tobias put his fingers in his ears but, obviously, he still heard us, and no way was he getting away. Once he realized that, he sprinted toward the deep end, screaming, his arms extended, and belly flopped into the pool. His body made the loudest smacking sound when he hit the surface, and I cringed just imagining the pain.

And I didn't have to imagine on my own because Tobias resurfaced and screamed his head off. He used some curse words that I couldn't repeat because they were not allowed at my house.

I glanced toward my mom and Ted, who were sitting on the patio drinking lemonade. They waved but didn't say anything, which was exactly what they were supposed to do. So far so good!

When Tobias climbed out of the pool, I couldn't help but notice his bright red tummy. "You okay?" I asked.

"So far I would say this is not the best birthday party I've ever been to," he said.

I shrugged. "Your fault for pushing in Joe."

Then I climbed down the ladder and into the pool.

Emma dived in, Claire cannonballed, and Yumi walked around to the steps at the shallow end. Now that we were all in, we played catch with a giant rainbow-striped beach ball. Then we played a couple of rounds of Marco Polo until Tobias got mad and accused everyone of cheating. And then the boys had a diving contest while Claire and Emma choreographed a dance routine to the new Katy Perry song. Yumi jumped out of the pool to text Nathan, and I treaded water with my hands in the air, timing myself to see how long I could last before sinking or using my arms.

And again I was thinking about how lucky I was to have a swimming pool. And all my awesome friends and how this was the best birthday I'd ever had in my whole entire life. And how summer was going to be filled with fun and pool parties and the Panda Parade, and my life could seriously not get any better. Then Rachel showed up.

I didn't even see her at first. I was out of the pool and about to jump in backward because Oliver had dared me to, and there she was—in jeans and a black T-shirt and her dark-green ski cap. She also wore giant tortoiseshell sunglasses.

"Hey there," I said, waving happily.

"Glad you're having so much fun without me!" said Rachel.

I couldn't see her eyes behind her glasses, but I imagined they were squinting at me with anger and annoyance. At least it seemed that way from the tone of her voice.

I started to shiver, so I crossed my arms over my chest. "Huh?" I asked, totally confused by her comment because she was the one who was late. Did she expect us to all sit around and wait for her before starting the party?

"My party started at noon," I said, glancing up at the outdoor clock. "You're almost an hour late."

"I'm sorry, but some of us had chores to do this

morning," she replied, all hostile, as if I'd been the one to make her do whatever it was she had to do.

I decided to ignore this comment. "Um, where's your bathing suit?" I asked.

"I forgot it," she said.

"Do you want to borrow one of mine?" I asked.

"No," Rachel said with a yawn. "I don't feel like swimming anyway."

"Okay," I said. And suddenly this unkind thought flashed into my brain: *I don't feel like dealing with your grumpy self.* I didn't say it out loud, though. Instead I jumped back into the pool without another word.

"You were supposed to go in backward," said Oliver.

"Oh yeah, I forgot," I said, swimming back to the steps so I could try it again. This time when I walked past Rachel, I ignored her. I heard her let out a little puff of air in frustration.

"Hey, Rachel, aren't you coming in?" Claire called.

"No," Rachel said.

I continued to swim and have fun at my party. Rachel wandered over to the shade and sat down cross-legged on the ground.

And a half an hour later Ted said he was firing up the barbecue. It was a good thing, too, because by the time the food was ready, I was starving.

I wrapped myself in a fluffy blue-and-yellow-striped towel and shivered as I bit into a delicious cheeseburger.

Oliver sat on one side of me and Claire was on the other.

Corn Dog Joe asked if there were any corn dogs, which surprised no one.

"I've only got regular dogs and veggie dogs with plain buns," Ted explained.

"No, thanks," said Joe. "I'll have a burger."

Rachel took a hamburger but hardly ate a thing. No chips, no salsa, no carrots, no nothing. She didn't even put mustard on the bun, which was weird because I'd never seen Rachel eat a hamburger without mustard.

"Are you okay?" asked Emma.

"Fine," said Rachel, staring at her burger and not touching it. "I'm just not hungry."

I didn't know why she came to the party if she wasn't going to swim and she wasn't going to eat much. It was like she was deliberately making herself have a rotten time. But I didn't bother saying so. I didn't even look at her.

After the rest of us finished, my mom came outside with the most beautiful birthday cake I'd ever seen. It had three tiers, and each level was a different color—green, pink, and light blue. It had yellow polka dots on the middle layer, and yellow stripes on the top and bottom layers. It looked like a fancy hat, the kind old ladies wear on Easter Sunday.

There was just one candle on top—a jumbo number twelve. The top layer of the cake read *Happy Birthday, Annabelle* in fancy calligraphy.

My friends sang "Happy Birthday" to me, and I blew out my candle.

Then my mom cut and served the cake.

Oliver, Tobias, and Joe wolfed their slices down and asked if they could have seconds.

"This is delicious and totally gorgeous," said Claire. "May I have another piece too?"

"Of course," said my mom.

"Hey, we should have a special birthday line of sock puppets, don't you think?" asked Emma. "Like, we can do special-order ones and charge extra money for them. Personally engraved."

"More than six dollars?" asked Yumi. "We don't even know if our new line is going to sell. And I thought we were going to retire after we make this next batch. You know, because by then we'll have enough money for the Panda Parade weekend."

"I know we're taking the summer off, but it's never too early to start thinking about next year," said Emma. "I'm sure we can save up for some other concert. Or maybe we can all take a trip to Disneyland."

"That sounds awesome!" said Claire.

"But let's get through the Panda Parade first," I said.

"Okay," said Emma.

"And speaking of birthday sock puppets," said

Claire as she pulled a sock puppet out of her back-pack. It had blond hair and brown eyes, and it wore a red T-shirt and dark blue capri jeans. The outfit looked a little familiar. So did the sock puppet. She had a little orange basketball attached to her right hand.

"Is that supposed to be me?" I asked.

Claire smiled and nodded and handed it over. On the bottom she'd written, *Happy Birthday, Annabelle! Yay for Turning Twelve—Finally!* in blue puffy paint.

"This is awesome," I said.

"Are you sure it's fancy enough for you?" asked Rachel.

Everyone at the table got really quiet and looked at Rachel. I'd almost forgotten she was still at the party—this was the first thing she'd said in a really long time, not to mention the rudest.

"What did you say?" I asked.

"Nothing," said Rachel.

I stood up. "No, I definitely heard you say something. Did you just ask if Claire's present was fancy enough?"

"Yeah," said Rachel. "I wanted to make sure, since all you talk about now is your new house and your new pool and your new iPhone."

"What are you talking about?" I asked, feeling slightly sick to my stomach. "It's an old iPhone. It used to belong to Ted. Remember? I've told you that, like, a million times."

"Whatever. It's still an iPhone," said Rachel.

"They're, like, hundreds of dollars. My mom doesn't even have an iPhone."

"What does that have to do with anything?" I asked.

"I'm just saying," said Rachel. "Ever since you've moved, you've had kind of an attitude."

"No," I said, standing up. "Ever since I've moved, *you've* had an attitude. And I can't believe you'd be so rude to me on my birthday."

"You're right." Rachel stood quickly and knocked over her chair, which clattered loudly onto the concrete. "Maybe I should go!"

"Maybe you should!" I yelled. "Because I didn't want you here ruining my birthday party anyway!"

Rachel stormed off as soon as my mom and Ted came back with a pitcher of lemonade.

"What's going on?" my mom asked.

"Nothing!" I shouted.

I looked to my friends. Everyone seemed shocked—too shocked to say anything. I felt hot tears build up behind my eyes, and before I could blink them back, they poured out.

I was crying.

I was crying in front of everyone on my birthday.

chapter sixteen
disaster zone

Everyone seemed to take my tears as a cue to leave. Oliver hugged me good-bye, whispering, "Call me later" in my ear.

"Happy Birthday," my friends said from the door. Except it sounded more like a question and the answer was obviously no.

Rachel had stormed out minutes before, and I kind of felt like I never wanted to see her again.

I squeezed my eyes shut tightly, wishing I could take back the last ten minutes. This was completely mortifying—the worst end to what had been an amazing day.

I ran upstairs and into my room, slamming the door behind me and plugging my "fancy" phone into my new speaker dock. I put on the Lobster Lips and cranked up the volume.

And a minute later I heard a knock on my door. It was my mom.

"Yeah?" I asked.

"Want to talk about it?" she asked as she came

into my room and eased herself down into my desk chair, moving slowly since her belly was so big.

"Nope," I said.

"Are you sure?"

I flopped down on my bed, faceup, and stared at the ceiling. "I need to be alone for a while."

"Well, I'm here if you need me," she said, standing up again and heading for the door.

Once she was gone, I tried reading an old Harry Potter novel, but I couldn't concentrate. Then I decided to clean out my closet, but that got pretty boring.

Over the next twenty minutes Claire, Emma, Oliver, and Yumi had all texted me to ask if I was okay, but I didn't feel like talking to anyone. Nor did I feel like moping around, alone in my room all night.

I turned off my phone and headed downstairs and asked if I could go on a bike ride.

"Go ahead," my mom said. She and Ted were cleaning up from the party. The half-eaten cake sat on the kitchen counter, surrounded by all the balloons I'd rejected. The sight of it made me want to cry all over again. I couldn't believe I'd been so worried about balloons when my real problems were so much bigger.

"Be back by six, though. Okay?" asked Ted.

"Sure," I said, heading out to the garage.

I got my bike and rode all the way to the lake. There was a path that went around the water, but you weren't supposed to ride bikes on it—it was a walking path only. Sometimes, though, you could get lucky and ride all you wanted and no one would say anything, and tonight was one of those nights, which was lucky for me because I really needed to let off some steam. It was a mile around, and I did three whole loops as fast as I could. The wind stung my eyes, causing them to tear up, or maybe I still had some crying to do left over from this afternoon. I couldn't tell.

On my fourth loop, I noticed someone following me.

He was a blond boy on a skateboard and he was getting closer.

"Hey, Annabelle!" he yelled.

It was Jackson, Rachel's big brother.

I pedaled harder and tried to outrace him, but Jackson was really fast. He'd been skating since he could walk, practically. At least that was what Rachel had told me back when we were friends.

"Hey, stop!" he yelled.

I ignored him.

"Yo, Annabelle. I'm talking to you!"

And I'm trying to avoid you and everyone in your whole entire family, I thought as I rode even faster. Except the wheels of his board were getting louder— Jackson was getting closer—and pretty soon he grabbed on to the bottom of my seat, forcing me to pull him along.

"Cut it out," I said as my bike wobbled. I didn't slow down, hoping he'd fall off. Except he didn't and he wouldn't let go. I tried weaving back and forth and made some sharp turns, but I just couldn't lose him.

"Just stop!" he yelled, and I braked hard, hoping he'd go flying, and he did—straight into me! As my bike tipped I lost my balance and fell down.

"Ow!" I yelled. "What the heck?"

"Sorry," said Jackson.

"What were you thinking?" I asked, standing up and checking out my knee, which was now bloody.

"That looks like it hurts," Jackson said.

I glared at him. "It does. A lot." He, I noticed, was completely unscathed. And pretty quiet, too, especially for someone who was so desperate to talk to me. "What's your deal?" I asked.

He took a deep breath and said, "We need to talk."

"Ever heard of a phone?" I asked.

"I don't have your number and Rachel wouldn't give it to me," he said, brushing his hands through his hair. "I stopped by your house and your mom said you went on a bike ride."

"How did you know I was here?" I asked.

Jackson shrugged. "I didn't. Lucky guess. I checked the park first and you weren't there."

"What do you want, anyway?"

"We're moving," he said.

"What are you talking about?" I asked.

He smirked and let out an angry sort of laugh. "Yeah, I figured Rachel didn't tell you."

"You're serious?" I asked. "Where are you going?"

"To my grandparents' house," he said.

Rachel and Jackson's grandparents live in Morrison Woods, just a few blocks away from my old house and Rachel's current house, but I didn't understand what was going on. Also, I couldn't believe that Rachel was acting so mad at me for moving when she was about to do the same thing. The hypocrisy made me even madder, something I didn't even think was possible.

"Why wouldn't she tell me?" I asked.

"Well, know how my dad lost his job last year?" he asked.

I shook my head. I didn't know any of this.

"Well, he did. And my mom works part time, but she doesn't make that much money, and my parents can't afford our house anymore. So we're going." Jackson shrugged and gave me a hard stare.

None of this made any sense and, to be honest, my mind was kind of blown. "What do you mean they can't afford the house? It's your house. You guys have lived there forever!"

"I know, since I was born. But now we won't. The bank owns it, really, is what my dad says. I don't know. It doesn't make sense, but my parents messed up and now we have to move."

"Well, where are your grandparents going?" I asked.

"Nowhere, dummy," said Jackson, squinting at me. "We're all going to be living in their house together."

It was mean of him to call me dummy, but I didn't say so. I was too busy processing all this new information. Could this news explain why Rachel had been acting weird? Because my family moved into a bigger house and her family was losing theirs?

I could see how it would be hard, watching your best friend get lots of new stuff when you were losing the only house you'd ever lived in.

But none of it was my fault or her fault or Jackson's. It was just what being a kid was all about—having grown-ups make all these big decisions for you.

"When did all of this happen?" I asked.

"About two months ago," said Jackson. "That's why I'm so surprised you don't know. Rachel's not great at keeping secrets. And you're her best friend."

I gulped, feeling a twinge of guilt, as I remembered the night of my first big sleepover. "Was it when you had that dinner at your grandparents? On a Saturday night? Like the day after I moved away? Is that when you found out?"

Jackson nodded. "Yeah, I think so. We had a big family meeting. Rachel and I thought we were going to discuss where to go for Christmas next year. Then instead everybody sprung this crazy plan on us. We had no idea any of this was happening."

"Wow, that stinks," I said.

"Yeah," said Jackson. "It's pretty messed up. Anyway, I just wanted you to know. If my sister's been weird lately—well, more weird than usual, I mean—there's a reason. We've gotta move, and when we get to my grandparents' house, we've got to share a room."

Before I could say another word, he skated off. As I watched his figure fade, tears came to my eyes.

I got home later than I was supposed to, I guess, because my mom and Ted were pretty upset.

"Why were you ignoring our calls?" my mom asked.

"What calls?" I wondered, as I checked my back pocket. "I don't have my phone with me."

"Is it lost?" asked Ted.

"We've been so worried," my mom added.

"I'm fine. My phone is probably upstairs."

I found it on my desk, and when I turned it on, I saw I had a gazillion text messages.

Claire wrote: *Call me!*

Emma wrote: *Are you okay???*

Yumi said: *Thanks 4 the party. Super-fun until the end* ☹

Oliver wrote: *My mom made ginger cookies. Come over if u want one.*

u home?

Want me to bring u a cookie?

Then Claire again: *Where are u?*

Annabelle?

Earth to Annabelle. Come in Annabelle.

Are u trapped in the bottom of a well?

Did u forget to plug in your phone?

What is going on?

WHERE R U?

The last text message on my phone was from Yumi, and it was more upsetting than anything. Here's what she wrote:

Claire and Emma and I talked about the Rachel-Annabelle situation. We won't take sides. We don't want u 2 to fight. We won't finish sock puppets without you. So if you don't make up, we can't go to the Panda Parade. ☹ ☹ ☹ ☹ ☹

I turned off my phone and dropped it onto the floor by my bed. I couldn't even begin to text back to anyone. What would I say? I couldn't believe I was in this situation. We'd all worked so hard. We had to go to the Panda Parade. I didn't want to let my friends down. But Rachel ruined my birthday party. Okay, she was going through a pretty bad time, but she could've told me. Instead she was mean to me, so why should I be the one to apologize? It wasn't fair.

Yet thinking about the whole big mess kept me up half the night.

chapter seventeen
clemson court reunion

First thing Sunday morning I got back on my bike and headed over to Rachel's house. It was my first time being there since the big move. I felt like I was the Ghost of Christmas Past, riding down Clemson Court, going back in time to my old life, when Rachel and I were best friends. When I was the new kid in town and Rachel knew everything.

Things sure were different now.

She'd said so many mean things, I was still pretty mad. But I'd also been up most of the night thinking about it all, and I kind of understood where she was coming from. Losing your house had to be awful. And having your friend move into a fancy new house just made things worse. I got that. But we were supposed to be best friends, so why didn't Rachel tell me what was going on? Was she embarrassed? And if so, why? What was there to be embarrassed about? Her parents' situation had nothing to do with her. Parents make all sorts of crazy decisions, and people moved all the time. Plus, Rachel wasn't even going very far. She'd still be in the neighborhood. I could still walk to her house. That was important. Not as good as what we used to have—I knew that. But it wouldn't be so bad. Of course, I wouldn't want to share a room with Jackson either. That was just one more lousy aspect. Although it was nice of Jackson to fill me in—even if he had to knock me over on my bike to do it.

When I got to Rachel's, I noticed someone on my lawn. My old lawn, I meant.

It was Sienna, Rachel's little friend. The one she took care of sometimes. The two of them were playing Four Square on the sidewalk. The court was drawn in blue chalk, the numbers etched in green.

When Rachel saw me, she stopped midhop. She didn't smile or say hello or anything, but she didn't ignore me either.

"Hi," I said, approaching carefully.

Before she said anything, Sienna tugged on her arm and said, "Rachel, it's your turn."

"I know," said Rachel. "I need to take a quick break, though. Okay?"

"Then I won this round," said Sienna, placing her hands on her hips and pouting a bit.

"Okay, that's fair," Rachel told her. "Let's go inside and get your mom, okay? I think you guys are heading out pretty soon."

"Wait, tell your friend about my swing," said Sienna.

Rachel turned to me and explained. "Sienna has a swing in her bedroom. Isn't that cool?"

"A real swing?" I asked.

She nodded. "My daddy hung it from the ceiling."

"You're lucky," I said.

"You can come over to my house too," said Sienna. "But you may be too big for the swing."

"Thanks," I said. "But we have some things to talk about. Maybe we can stop by another time. Okay?"

"Promise?" asked Sienna.

As I nodded, Sienna's mom came outside and joined us. She was carrying something lumpy in a sling wrapped around her chest. When she got closer, I saw it was a baby.

"Sienna, are you a big sister?" I asked.

She nodded proudly. "I am. That's baby June."

"That's awesome. Give me five," I said, holding up my hand.

Sienna jumped and gave me some skin.

"I'm going to be a big sister soon too. My mom is having a baby in two months."

Sienna looked at me suspiciously. "Aren't you kind of old for that?" she asked.

I laughed. "Old for being a big sister? Um, no one's ever asked me that before. But no. I'm not."

"Okay," Sienna said, but from the way she drew out the word, I could tell she didn't believe me.

"Sienna's from Australia," Rachel told me as we crossed the street. "That's why she says 'mum' instead of 'mom.'"

Now that we were alone, I decided to cut right to the chase. "Jackson tracked me down last night and told me you guys were moving," I said.

Rachel huffed out a breath, annoyed. "My brother should mind his own business."

"It is his business," I said. "It affects your whole family, right?"

"Well, yeah. Obviously. But I can't believe he told you," said Rachel.

"I can't believe you didn't."

"We weren't supposed to tell anyone. My mom told us not to," said Rachel. "She said we shouldn't air our dirty laundry and that doesn't mean we shouldn't wear old clothes. Because that's what I thought at first, and Jackson would never go for that. Haven't you noticed how he's worn the same blue nylon shorts practically every single day this month?"

"I thought he had a bunch of pairs that looked the same," I said.

"Nope." Rachel shook her head. "They're the same ones. He wears them for a few days until my mom insists on washing them, and then he puts them right back on again. He doesn't let her wash them too often because he doesn't want them getting worn-out."

"That's funny," I said, smiling. I felt the same way

about my favorite pair of jeans, and I was surprised to have this or anything in common with Jackson. I decided to keep this discovery to myself.

"Anyway, it's not definite. We may be able to keep the house, and I've been trying to help out. I take care of Sienna sometimes when her mom's busy with the baby. She pays me, and I've been saving all the money. I made fifty dollars this month."

Suddenly something occurred to me. "Is that why you're not contributing money to the Panda Parade fund?" I asked.

Rachel nodded. "We were doing so well with the sock puppets, and I figured my parents needed the money more. That was my plan, anyway. I gave it to my mom because I thought it would help us stay in the house and I thought she'd be all happy, but it turned into a disaster."

"What do you mean?" I asked. "Wasn't she glad you were trying to help out?"

"Well, I brought it to dinner and handed it to them, and my parents looked at it, and my dad got this horrible expression on his face. Like he was mad and humiliated and wanted to be anywhere else. I've seriously never seen him like that. It was awful. But my mom? She was even worse. My mom started crying. And then Jackson started yelling at me and he called me dumb because my parents need fifty *thousand* dollars, which I could never make taking care of Sienna. And seeing my mom cry and having Jackson be all mean and my dad acting so uncomfortable, it made me cry too, and so the entire night was ruined. Kind of like my life will be if we have to move."

By the time Rachel finished telling me all this, there were tears in her eyes and I felt like crying too.

I gave her a hug and said, "I had no idea this was going on. I wish you'd told me."

"Probably I should've. It's awkward. Promise me you won't tell our other friends."

"I promise," I said. "But we've got to make things right. Otherwise no Panda Parade."

"That would be awful," Rachel agreed. "I'm sorry I ruined your birthday party. It's not your fault you got to move into a fancy house."

"It's not," I said. "But I think it's okay for me to like my new house. And with the jean jacket and the new phone too . . . I never meant to rub those things in. They just sort of happened, and I don't think I need to be embarrassed about them."

"True, but it's hard for me because you get so much new stuff all the time," said Rachel.

"But who cares?" I asked. "It's all just stuff. What people have—it doesn't make them who they are. You know that. My mom always says that how you treat people is the most important thing. And like with the Panda Parade. It's fun to make money, but it's also just fun to be all together making the sock puppets, and it's fun to have created a successful business."

Rachel nodded. "Yeah. I know what you mean."

"Everyone is counting on us to make up and get back to work," I said. "They all got together and texted me and said we had to or no sock puppets, which means no Panda Parade and that would be the worst."

"Yeah, they texted me the same thing," said Rachel.

"It would stink to drop out now, when we're so close."

"You're right. I've been unfair and I'm sorry." Rachel kicked at the ground with the toe of her sneaker. "Can we forget about it? Please?"

"I hope you don't have to move," I said. "But even if you do—you'll still go to the same school and we'll still be best friends."

Rachel looked up at me and asked, "You still want to be best friends with me after I've been so mean?"

"You apologized," I said. "And you're going to stop. Right?"

Rachel gave me a hug. "Of course!"

"Should I call everyone and tell them we're cool?" I asked.

Rachel grinned. "Definitely!"

We spent the rest of the day at Claire's and finished our final round of sock puppets, tricking them out like never before.

When we got to school on Monday, we announced this was our final sale and word spread fast. We were mobbed, and sold out in record time.

Back at Claire's we counted our cash.

"You guys, we made more than a thousand dollars!" said Emma.

"We can get tickets *and* T-shirts," said Yumi. "And probably even—"

"Can we take a helicopter there?" asked Claire, interrupting.

Everyone cracked up.

"I'm serious!" said Claire.

"Not quite," said Emma.

"Well, maybe we should make puppets for another few weeks," said Claire. "And really go for it."

I shook my head and said, "Let's quit while we're ahead."

"No, let's just get our tickets," said Emma. "Immediately!"

To which there was nothing to do but cheer.

chapter eighteen
at long last, the panda parade

School was out. Summer was here. And before we knew it, fourth of July weekend had arrived.

"I have amazing news," Rachel said, grinning like crazy as she climbed into the van. She was the last person we picked up on our trip around Westlake. Claire, Yumi, Emma, and I were already in the car. "We don't have to move!"

"Are you serious?" I asked.

Rachel nodded.

"Move where?" asked Claire.

"Yeah, what are you talking about?" asked Yumi.

"It's a long story," said Rachel, explaining everything in a rush. "We were almost going to have to move but now we don't have to because my dad got a new job and then my grandparents decided to sell their house and lend us some money. They were moving in a few years anyway, when my grandfather retires. They said they'd sell now and move into a smaller place. And now that my dad has a job, he can pay them back over the next few years, so everything is okay."

"That's amazing!" I said, giving her a hug. "I am so happy you don't have to move!"

"Yeah, me too! We should celebrate," said Rachel. "I have an idea—let's go to Indio for the weekend. I hear there's this awesome benefit concert thing happening."

All of us cracked up. Now that we were together, we could finally be on our way.

Claire's mom Vanessa was driving, and Yumi's mom, Yoko, was the other chaperone. They sat in the front seat, leaving the rest of the car to us.

Minivans are basically living rooms on wheels, as far as I'm concerned. So even though we hit a ton of traffic and the drive down took more than three hours, it wasn't so bad. We were having our own party. I sat in the way, way back on the bench seat in the middle.

Rachel was on my right. Claire was on my left. Yumi and Emma were in the bucket seats in the middle, but the seats were swivel chairs so we were all facing one another. We had snacks, we had awesome music, and yes, we had to keep our seat belts on, but we were still able to do some pretty awesome minivan-seated choreography.

"Oh, I love this song!" Claire said, clapping as the new Lorde song came on.

"Me too!" I agreed.

"When do you think she's going to perform?" asked Claire.

"Hopefully first," said Yumi.

"I think they save the best acts for last," said Rachel.

"Isn't Katy Perry the best?" asked Emma.

"No, Taylor Swift for sure," said Claire.

"I think they're equally amazing," I said.

"I guess it doesn't matter who's first since we're going to get to see everyone," said Yumi.

When Yoko called, "We're here!" we all screamed.

As soon as Vanessa parked, we scrambled out of the van and joined the tremendous line. It seemed to snake on forever.

"I need to pee," said Claire.

"You can't pee now," said Emma. "There's nowhere to go until we get inside."

"This line is crazy," said Yumi.

"It's moving fast, at least," said Rachel.

"I hope we don't miss anything," I said.

"Don't worry, girls," said Vanessa. "These things never start on time."

"And you'll still hear the music from out here even if we haven't gotten inside the gates," Yoko said. She probably meant to reassure us, but the thought of not getting inside in time sounded too awful to bear!

I had my ticket in my hand, but I got sweaty and the ticket got damp and I was afraid that maybe a damp ticket wouldn't be valid anymore.

"What's wrong?" Rachel asked, because I guess she noticed me fidgeting.

"Nothing," I said. "I just can't believe we're really here. It's unreal, you know? We've been looking forward to this day for so long. I keep waiting for something to go wrong."

"Like the tickets won't work," said Claire.

"Exactly, because mine's all wet." I showed her the damp piece of paper.

"Except they will. Don't worry," said Yumi, squeezing my hand. "Wow, you are sweaty."

"Told you so!"

When the moment finally came, I handed over my ticket, half expecting the ticket taker to congratulate me, because getting here hadn't been easy.

We'd sold almost two hundred sock puppets. We'd suffered through fights and squabbles and bee stings and severely chapped lips and I'd even accidentally stapled the sleeve of my favorite shirt to a sock puppet.

I figured there'd be some sort of acknowledgment about the hardships we'd endured and everything we'd accomplished. Except she simply scanned my ticket with her little scanner and handed it back to me and said, "Enjoy."

"I will," I said.

My friends and I walked through the gates and looked around. The place was mobbed!

"I've never seen so many people in one place!" Rachel shouted over the noise.

I had to agree. The place was huge and there were people everywhere. I kept getting jostled by random people and really had to focus on not losing my friends. There was a gigantic stage straight ahead, except we were so far away, the people looked like tiny toy figurines.

There were four other stages—smaller ones—two on each side. And lots of booths in the middle selling T-shirts and french fries and popcorn and burritos.

I checked my watch. It wasn't yet noon. We still had time.

"Let's wander," said Claire, linking her arm through mine.

"Hold on a second!" said Yumi's mom. "We need a plan. You girls need to stick together. No one can go off by themselves. If you need to go to the bathroom— take a friend. If you need to get a snack—take a friend. We are going to meet at this flagpole every hour. Everyone understand?"

"You mean you're not coming with us?" Claire asked, her eyes bright.

Vanessa put her arm around Claire's shoulders. "We discussed this with everyone's parents and decided you girls are old enough to be on your own. As long as you check in with us every hour."

Yoko pointed to the flagpole in the center of the field. "You'll be able to see the check-in spot from wherever you are."

I couldn't believe we were going to get to wander around by ourselves. It was thrilling and scary and amazing we were old enough to do this.

We got popcorn, and elbowed our way as close to

the front of the stage as we could get. There were teenagers and old people and every age in between.

"We still have ten minutes. Maybe we should walk around some more!" Yumi shouted over the noise.

"But then we'd give up this spot," said Emma.

Suddenly a loud clap of thunder boomed across the sky.

"Wow, that was so loud, I felt it in my bones," I said, covering my hands with my ears.

The crowd let out a huge moan of disappointment.

"It cannot rain," said Emma. "We worked too hard to get here. It cannot rain!"

Except as Emma said this, the skies seemed to open up and the rain came pouring down in giant sheets.

We ran for shelter, except there was so little. Just one area near the food where they'd constructed a gigantic wooden overhang, and everyone seemed to have the same idea that we had.

"The concert cannot be canceled," yelled Claire.

My face was soaking wet, so you couldn't have seen the tears. Three businesses, three months, a three-hour car ride, and here we were. Claire was right—the concert could not be canceled. The universe couldn't do that to us!

I glanced at my watch. At twelve o'clock, precisely, the rain let up, as if by magic, or through the sheer force of our collective wills.

The clouds drifted away and the sun came out.

The ground was soaked and there were giant puddles everywhere, but none of us cared. We grabbed hands and ran back to the stage and ended up in an even better spot than before.

Soon a woman in a navy-blue suit came out to talk about the pandas.

"Thanks to your help, more than one million dollars have been raised to help the pandas!" she yelled.

"Yay!" We all clapped.

And then the lights dimmed and the spotlight shined in the center of the stage and out she came. The crowd roared so loudly, my ears hurt. We were in the center of everything!

We were shaking with excitement and shivering from cold and soaked through to our underwear, and I didn't know where the shivering stopped and the shaking began, but it didn't matter. This was our moment.

As the first band stepped onto the stage, fireworks shot through the sky. And when the lead singer began to sing, I felt just about ready to explode with excitement.

I could give you a play-by-play, list every single song that every single band played. Show you all the dance moves. But it wouldn't do the night justice. It was simply something you had to be there for, the kind of experience that was impossible to re-create. In a word: perfection. In two words: pure bliss.

I was twelve and so were my four best friends. We

were at the concert of our dreams. When it ended, we'd still have the entire summer to look forward to. Life was awesome. In fact, it was beyond awesome.

Well, except for the disaster that happened right before Labor Day. But that's a story for next time!